Mattie's Call

Dear Reader:

Stacy Campbell spent summers in Georgia listening to stories told by older relatives on the porch. With her fourth novel, she makes the reader feel they are sitting next to her as she spins this Southern, heart-warming tale of family values.

Mattie Benson, a mother of three, walks away from a nursing home and a Mattie's Call is issued. Her estranged adult children, Gabrielle, Alice and Joshua, are forced to make amends while they search for their missing mom, whom they had abandoned. Once she is considered deceased, they discover she has left specific requests in her will that each must follow before they are allowed any inheritance. We watch how the siblings comply with her requests and manage to reconnect with each other.

It's all about family and bonding; about ensuring you treasure each moment with your parents and loved ones. The book is filled with messages that will open one's eyes about being appreciative of relatives while they are alive. Stacy keeps us turning pages with the many twists and offers us food for thought until the very end.

Her third novel, *Wouldn't Change a Thing*, deals with mental illness, another topic that is often swept under the rug among families.

As always, thanks for supporting the authors of Strebor Books. We always try to bring you groundbreaking, innovative stories that will entertain and enlighten. I can be located at www.facebook.com/AuthorZane or reached via email at Zane@eroticanoir.com.

Blessings,

Zane

Publisher
Strebor Books
www.simonandschuster.com

ALSO BY STACY CAMPBELL

Wouldn't Change a Thing

Forgive Me

Dream Girl Awakened

ZANE PRESENTS

Mattie's Call

A NOVEL

STACY CAMPBELL

STREBOR BOOKS
NEW YORK LONDON TORONTO SYDNEY

Strebor Books
P.O. Box 6505
Largo, MD 20792
http://www.streborbooks.com

This book is a work of fiction. Names, characters, places and incidents are products of the author's imagination or are used fictitiously. Any resemblance to actual events or locales or persons, living or dead, is entirely coincidental.

ISBN 978-1-59309-600-7
ISBN 978-1-4767-7734-4 (ebook)
LCCN 2015957692

First Strebor Books trade paperback edition April 2016

Cover design: www.mariondesigns.com
Cover photograph: © Keith Saunders/Keith Saunders Photos

10 9 8 7 6 5 4 3 2 1

Manufactured in the United States of America

This book is dedicated to my wonderful friends at a local nursing home. They asked me not to name the facility or give their names, but they asked me to tell my readers if you have a living parent or parents and you're not getting along, repair the broken relationships, spend time together, and tie up all your loose ends before it's too late.

1
Only My Last Name

"My children are a waste of tears and stretch marks!"

"Ms. Mattie, you don't mean that."

"Karen, you heard me and I mean every word." Mattie eyed her watch for the ninth time. "Gigi knows today is Emma's memorial service. Bad enough they put me in this place. The least she could do is pick me up on time. I don't want to walk in late."

Karen readjusted Mattie's hat, tilting it to the left the way she liked. "Give me her number. I'll try again."

Mattie gave Karen her phone. "Be my guest. You'll need pixie dust and unicorns to make her answer."

Karen scrolled through the contacts and found the number. She dialed, listening to a song that played forever. When prompted she said, "Ms. Gabrielle, this is Karen Ball, Ms. Mattie's CNA from Grand Oak Acres. Please call your mother ASAP. She's waiting for you to take her to Ms. Emma's funeral."

She waited for Karen to end the call. "She's not calling back."

"We don't know that." Karen shifted the conversation. "You look good in your black tweed suit, Ms. Mattie. Spiffy as all get-out!"

"Hand me my gloves from the top drawer."

"Yes, ma'am."

Mattie smoothed out her suit. It was a gift from Emma after they finally made a pact to get along. They bonded over the realization their children had put them out to pasture, deciding they were ancient as eight-tracks and pagers. She placed the gloves on her lap.

"These were the last pair of gloves my husband, Daniel, bought me before he passed. Feel the lining."

Karen felt the rabbit fur and handed them back to Mattie. "Those are nice. And expensive, I bet."

"Daniel bought most of my clothes. He said we represented each other and should look good. He felt the same way about the children. Appearance mattered to him, and he believed the first impression people had of you stuck. He'd be so ashamed of how our children are acting." Mattie gazed out the window, sighed, and fidgeted with her watch again.

"Do you want me to call Joshua?"

"He doesn't get off work 'til four."

"How about Alice?"

"Jim Jones won't let her come pick me up."

"Jim Jones?"

"That's what I call my bossy, controlling son-in-law. You remember the Jonestown, Guyana, massacre? The preacher who conned all the folks out of money and property. They moved to—" Mattie paused. "Karen, how old are you?"

"Twenty-four."

"You never heard about Jonestown?"

"No ma'am."

"What's the thing you all do for information?" Mattie snapped her fingers in rapid clicks. "Google. Google him."

Mattie's phone trilled. She had insisted Karen set her alarm and ringtone to the old phone tune. Mattie's connection to her past depended on nostalgia, and the ring tone reminded her of the phone that rang in their Colonial when the kids were younger. Karen held the phone to her ear, but Mattie pushed her hand away.

"I don't want to talk to Gigi. Tell her I said hurry up!"

Karen sat on Emma's bed. "Ms. Gabrielle, are you near?" She nodded and smiled as Gabrielle spoke. "I'll bring her to the lobby in fifteen minutes. See you soon."

Mattie frowned. "What's her excuse today?"

"She got caught up at the mall. She said she was getting you a Christmas gift."

"I'll believe it when I see it."

Karen wanted to lighten Mattie's mood. She made the mistake of calling Gabrielle "Gigi" once and was told to never address her by the pet name her father gave her. Her presence stirred too many negative emotions in Mattie, and she never knew how to handle the matter. Karen heard eggshells cracking at the mention or sight of Gabrielle. "I'll get your coat so we can move up front."

Mattie stood. "I can get my own coat. I'm not an invalid, you know."

Used to her Gabrielle-induced snappy tone, she placated her with, "You've got so many pretty coats, I wanted to make sure we picked the best one."

"Flattery will get you everywhere with me. Especially these days."

A pall of sadness covered Mattie's face. She plopped down on Emma's bed, missing her friend more each day. Since her roommate's death, she hoped Watford or Amelia—Emma's son and daughter—would call to say there'd been a mistake. She wanted them to say paramedics had resuscitated Emma and she would come back to Grand Oak. Her children left her clothes and personal items at the nursing home, insisting they'd pick them up after the service. Mattie eyed the photo of the two of them at the Gullah Festival. They stood between two female stilt walkers, faces painted, clutching dangling beads, and smiling for Joshua. He'd taken the day off to drive them to Beaufort for the festivities. She blinked back tears staring at Emma; the face painting was Emma's idea.

"Ms. Mattie, the wool coat matches your outfit—" The trail of tears made Karen drop Mattie's coat on a chair. She sat next to her, rubbing her shoulders. "Don't cry. It's going to be okay. Ms. Emma's in a better place now."

"And where is that? Playing harps and eating grapes in heaven?"

Karen embraced Mattie tighter. "I didn't mean anything bad by what I said."

Mattie's bunched shoulders relaxed. "I'm sorry for snapping. You young folk don't know what it's like to lose your family members one by one, or have family that doesn't see about you. I see your daddy dropping lunch off for you sometimes when I'm sitting in the lobby."

"He is a good dad to me and my brother."

"You can count the number of times on half a hand Emma's children came to see about her. Mine aren't much better. Sometimes I feel like they have only my last name."

"What does that mean?"

"My grandmother used to say after some families became adults, the only thing they had in common were their last names. Divided, not fellowshipping, not seeing after one another."

"How morbid."

"I know. I never believed it either until my kids..." Her voice trailed off and she took Karen's right hand in hers. "Promise me you'll stay as close to your brother as you can. Your parents too."

"I'll try. We take trips and spend time together. The only reason I'm working here is because I realized being a CNA isn't enough to have the kind of life I want. I'm back in school now. This helps me pay tuition."

"Good. If I could convince my other daughter, Alice, to go back to school, I'd be on cloud nine."

"What's stopping her?"

"Jim Jones."

Mattie and Karen doubled over in a fit of giggles.

"Is your son-in-law *that* bad?"

"After Alice married Beryl, she was chained to suburbia. The child I raised died at the reception. Sure, Beryl is a big-time businessman, but she handed herself over to him on a silver platter in the name of Jesus. I've never seen two people go through so many religions. First they were Christians, then Catholics. After that, they've been everything in between. The last time we talked, they were into some long-name faith I can't pronounce. I don't know who she is anymore, and neither does she. Humph, every religion though, he's the leader."

Karen, guilty that she'd spun up Mattie, said, "Your son seems nice. He's older, but he's so good-looking."

"He is. Always was a loner, though. Handsome as all get-out. You can hear panties dropping when he walks in a room. Gigi is my smartest child, but Josh is the most determined one. He's an aeronautical engineer and a runaway groom. Been engaged more times than I can count."

"They are some characters. Ms. Gabrielle is the most exciting one of all of them."

"She's a spoiled brat who should have been disciplined as a child. She's gotten through life on her looks. They're fading and she doesn't know it. A woman's dance is soon over, and with this age-obsessed society, she was old at thirty. She's forty-nine, Joshua is forty, and Alice is thirty-eight. See how long it took me to have a baby after Gigi? Nine whole years. Daniel spoiled her rotten and I've been paying for it ever since."

"Let's get this coat on you so we can get you to the lobby, Ms. Mattie."

"I told you I can put my own coat on," Mattie said, playfully patting Karen's hand away as she stood. "The repast is at the community center on Tybee Island. I'm sure you'll be gone when I come back."

"If you don't mind, bring me back an obit. You and Ms. Emma are like second grandmothers to me."

Mattie winked. "I'll see what I can do."

"Don't forget to take your aspirin with you. Your headaches have been coming more frequently. I worry about you, Ms. Mattie."

She shook her purse, making sure the pills rattled. "I'll outlive you. I'm a tough old bird."

"Tell me anything."

Mattie looked at herself in the full-length mirror. Her soft, roller-set, cherrywood hair glimmered thanks to her standing appointment with Kennedy, the stylist responsible for reopening the nursing home salon. Her curls flowed beyond her hat. Vanity made her fall under the Clairol spell every four weeks after Kennedy asked her to choose between the colors Cherrywood or Silken Black. After they'd aged, Daniel didn't like her hair black; said coloring it made her look like she was trying to be young. He suggested she explore red or auburn tones which complemented her skin color. As she turned left, she caught a glimpse of Gigi in the doorway. The floor-length fur she donned was too heavy for December, especially in Savannah, Georgia. Mattie was sure the coat was a gift from her non-working child's latest sponsor. Gigi's tousled curls flowed, and no doubt she'd spent hours seated at the upstairs vanity achieving the flawless makeup set. Mattie breathed, attempted to be kind for what was sure to be a painful afternoon.

"Gigi, I'm glad you—"

"Come on, Mama! You were supposed to be in the lobby. I have other things to do than chauffeur you around all day!"

2
Don't Ask Me Again

Mattie rode in silence as Gabrielle tapped her French manicured nails on the steering wheel. The sleek Mercedes in which they rode replaced the Cayenne she'd seen three months ago. A quick glance in the backseat revealed a bounty of gift-wrapped boxes. Her latest benefactor was generous. *He'll drop her soon like all the rest.*

"You have a lot of love to put under the tree this year, Gigi."

"I would've put a bigger dent in the love if I didn't have to pick you up today."

"Still disrespectful."

"What's disrespectful about being called at the *last minute* to take you to a funeral when I had plans?"

"I'm your mother, Gigi. Your seventy-two-year-old mother!"

"Mama, why are you at Grand Oak in the first place?"

Mattie looked out the window. Being reminded of her slip-ups by her oldest child produced cringe-worthy moments she tried to avoid. She closed her eyes, knowing Gigi would recount them like the alphabet.

"Oh, let me remind you, since the cat yanked out your tongue!"

"Gigi, don't."

"The small kitchen fire you set after warming up hot dogs and pork-and-beans."

"I was hungry and you left me in my own house for hours with no food. Bonita was generous enough to share those dogs and beans with me."

"Hmmm, what about the time you drove around the corner, mistook the accelerator for the brake, and plowed into Mr. Shipley's backyard garden? You're lucky his pit bull, Tyson, didn't maul you."

"I paid for his vegetables and replaced the garden boxes. You all didn't have to take away my keys."

Gabrielle removed her right hand from the wheel, fished in the backseat for a tall, square pink box, still balancing the car and wearing a smirk. She thrust the box at Mattie.

"Open it."

Mattie's delicate, age-spotted hands fiddled with the box and decorative bow. She opened it, silently praying it contained an assortment of her favorite snacks. As she pulled back the white tissue paper, the sight mortified her. The Depend bed protectors produced a deep intake of breath.

"They probably don't have quality bed pads at the nursing home, and I wanted to make sure you had the best."

"What makes you think I need these?"

"You're playing coy now?"

"What are you talking about, Gigi?"

"Joshua's girlfriend, Marilyn, said you wet the guest bedroom bed. They aren't angry or anything, but it got me to thinking about the pads and your incontinence."

Embarrassed, Mattie sank in her seat. She'd forgotten about that night at Joshua's five months ago. He and Marilyn had taken her to River Street and enjoyed a meal of steamed crab legs and corn-on-the-cob. They shopped at a few boutiques and chucked bills into trumpet and saxophone cases of young men and women entertaining passersby. The wonder and beauty of the night culminated into a dream about Daniel. In it, they were young again, living in the house he worked so hard to purchase, raising their three kids, and enjoying a Friday night game of Bid Whist with their best friends and neighbors, Bonita and Lou. Gigi ordered Joshua and Alice around, bossing them off the top of the stairs and making them bring snacks to the card table. The memories overwhelmed Mattie as she slept. The glass of wine she'd had on River Street tap danced on her bladder; warm urine trickled down her legs, ruining the expensive mattress in Joshua's guest bedroom.

In the softest tone, she muttered, "It was an accident, Gigi."

Gabrielle sighed and looked askance at her frail mother. Gone was the strong woman who accompanied her to Girl Scout meetings, band practice, and track meets. She wanted to have a better relationship with her, but her mother was a traitor. Mattie's first betrayal was giving birth to Joshua and Alice. She was content being an only child, but her parents ruined her peace by having those brats. Birth control pills were created well before she was born, and she wished her mother had taken them *after* she was born. Her second betrayal was letting her father die. The sun rose and set on Daniel Benson, and she was never convinced her mother's refusal to get a third opinion about his prostate cancer didn't contribute to his death.

"Did you hear me, Gigi?"

"What did you say?"

"The rotation. When are you all going to start the rotation again? If not for four months, one month. I want a break from the home sometimes."

Gabrielle huffed. Joshua devised the rotation two years before Mattie's admittance to Grand Oak. They took turns caring for her four months a year. The rotation gave them time with her while allowing the other siblings a break. They pooled their resources, hired a home health care nurse, and spent time with Mattie as best they could. The setup grew complicated as Joshua's work schedule increased, Alice refereed shouting matches between Mattie and Beryl, and Gigi's disappearing acts stretched out for days.

"Mama, we're all too busy to take care of you."

"Gigi, you don't work."

"I have a full day of activities."

"With Emma gone—"

"We're not doing it, so don't ask me again!"

Gabrielle followed a blue pickup truck into the parking lot of El Bethel Baptist Church. Judging the crowd milling around the front steps of the church, they'd made it to the service on time.

"Mama, we need to make this quick. I'm meeting one of my friends for dinner tonight."

"Gigi, the repast is on Tybee. I want to at least fellowship with her family before I leave. Eat a little something."

"I can get you some food on the way back to the home."

Mattie folded her arms. Exasperated, she recalled Gigi's eagerness to put her in Grand Oak Acres. She was all too happy to be granted Durable Power of Attorney over her affairs. Not only did Gigi sign the papers like a Hollywood starlet giving an autograph, she waved the representative payee form after being added to the bank and investment accounts. She shifted assets in her name to "protect" Mattie from being fleeced at Grand Oak. Only the house remained in Joshua's name; it was Daniel's death-bed request. Jewelry, priceless coins, and cash were tucked in a safe deposit box at their family bank. Every month, Gigi made sure Mattie had three-hundred dollars cash for incidentals.

"Gigi, I need you to do me a favor."

"What?"

"I need you to get something from the safe deposit box for me."

"What do you need?"

"My wedding rings. The last set Daniel bought me. Matter of fact, I'd like all my jewelry and the other items locked there."

"Those are too expensive to be worn in the home. What if someone steals them?"

"Karen protects everything for me."

Gabrielle paused, tapped the steering wheel again. "I'll see what I can do, Mama."

3
An Old-Fashioned Homegoing

Mattie stepped into the vestibule, marveling at the well-preserved edifice. El Bethel's Senior Outreach Ministry sent a van to Grand Oak every Sunday for residents who wanted to attend the eight o'clock service. She and Emma dressed in their finest and enjoyed the preaching style of Dr. Marcus Thornton. She felt lonely as she scanned the building's stained-glass windows, patchwork-quilt ceiling, and two teakwood benches—preserved from El Bethel's meetings during the Civil Rights Movement—nestled in the entryway. The building fund thermometer had moved significantly since the last time she visited. She stopped attending after Emma's last hospital admittance two months ago. She waved to her hall mates, Agatha, Corneila, and Harriet, huddled in a semicircle. Corneila and Harriet's rapt attention focused on Agatha. Had she known they were attending Emma's funeral, she would have asked for a ride and been spared Gigi's humiliating taunts. Then again, Agatha's grandson, BoPeep, drove a car that reeked of beer and marijuana. Agatha called him Peep and was gracious enough to share him with the ladies at Grand Oak as an ad hoc taxicab. Gabrielle clasped Mattie's hand and walked beside her, pretending to care. She did this when five or more people were gathered and didn't want to show her true colors. Agatha motioned them over.

Agatha held court in El Bethel just as she did at Grand Oak.

Freshly healed from a bout of pneumonia, she was back to her gossiping ways. Her hands moved a mile a minute; ever so often she'd push back her soft, silvery curls and continue the conversation. Behind her back, the residents said there wasn't a death that happened in Savannah that Agatha didn't know about. She knew the cause and perpetrator before the body hit the ground. She paused the conversation, zeroing in on Gabrielle's coat as they approached her.

"Oh, great. Biddy City," Gabrielle uttered.

"What, Gigi?"

"Nothing, Mama."

Agatha closed in the space between them. "That is some kind of coat, young lady. What is it, lynx?" Agatha, wearing her own mink stole, caressed the floor-length coat as if petting a small child. "I always wanted one of these. I know that set you back at least ten grand."

Soaking up the adoration, Gabrielle shimmied, refusing to divulge the price. "It was a gift from a friend."

"If I could turn back the hands of time, I'da found some friends like that when I was your age."

Mattie bristled at the thought of what her child did to get presents. She turned to Agatha. "We all sitting together?"

Corneila and Harriet looked annoyed but didn't speak.

"You missed the service. We're waiting now to see if the repast is still on Tybee Island."

"Over? What do you mean it's over? Gigi was a little late, but the service shouldn't be over." Mattie looked at her watch. "We still have twelve minutes before the service starts."

"You're deafer than a cobra, Mattie Benson. I'm trying to tell you Emma's selfish son and daughter had her cremated. Ain't no Batesville in the sanctuary!" Agatha pulled the stole closer and licked her lips. "On top of that, some ole preacher who wasn't Emma's got up in the pulpit, read a few scriptures, and gave the benediction."

"No!" Mattie waited for Agatha to revise her tale.

"As I live and breathe, that's exactly what they did!"

Mattie fished in her purse and removed the handwritten order of service Emma wrote out the night they watched *The Twilight Zone* marathon. Emma wanted an old-fashioned homegoing service. The upbeat solo, "We've Come to Praise His Name," was to be sung instead of "Precious Lord." She wanted the congregation to rejoice her ascent to heaven. She'd jotted down favorite scriptures and requested Pastor Corey Rountree, the newly installed leader of Angelic Arms Baptist Church, perform the eulogy. He had prayed with Emma and visited with her during numerous hospital visits. Family and friends would be allowed two minutes to share life reflections, and the repast would be in the church basement so people wouldn't have to drive far. Mattie had given Emma's son a copy the week before she died.

"My granddaughter, Zoe, the runner-up on season two of *Sunday Best*, usually charges one-fifty for solos. She was going to sing for free at Emma's service, and she wasn't given a chance," Agatha said, slicing through Mattie's sadness.

Gabrielle eyed Agatha and pursed her lips. The vision of Zoe prostituting her gift came to mind. She opened her mouth to say those very words, but instead offered, "Maybe it was too painful for her children to sit through a sad service."

"Painful my—" Agatha remembered where they were. "That son of hers is trying to get back to the racetrack and her daughter's waiting on the inheritance. They didn't wait until her body was cold before they started dividing the spoils." She looked to Mattie for support. When Mattie didn't respond, she continued, "You know as well as I do Emma didn't want to be cremated. She wanted all her pieces intact when she met her maker. She wanted a soloist and a nice spread in the basement. So much food people could take plates home."

"Let me find her son. There must have been some mix-up," said Mattie. Gabrielle followed her mother through the maze of hob-nobbing mourners.

They entered the sanctuary, said hello to familiar faces, and spotted Emma's children talking to a man so tall he could kiss heaven. He folded and unfolded his arms as he ran his fingers through his gray hair. He extended one arm upward, then pulled it down. The tailored suit he wore accentuated his large frame. Mattie recognized him immediately; Emma's brother, Clarence. They were in an earshot of the conversation and stood back as his fury gained momentum.

"This is wrong, Watford! My sister wouldn't have wanted things to end this way. How could you do this to her?"

Watford rolled his eyes and clucked his tongue. "Uncle Clarence, there were considerations."

"Such as?"

Amelia interrupted her brother. "Cremation is cheaper than embalming. Mama was low-key. We didn't need all the fanfare. Soloists. All that food. People droning on for hours about how wonderful she was. Where were they when she was alive?"

"Probably nearer than the two of you. I'm ashamed to call the two of you kin."

Watford pulled the unbuttoned suit jacket close to his rotund figure. Emma always said her son was digging his grave with his teeth with all the healthy portions he devoured. His face reddened at his uncle's words. "We gave Mama a decent burial. What's the problem?"

Clarence advanced three steps, coming nose to nose with his

nephew. "The problem is, you call me in New York less than forty-eight hours before a funeral to tell me my sister is dead. I get here, and not only is her body *not here* so I can look at her one last time, but my ignorant niece and nephew don't have bird sense to give their mother a Southern homegoing. Do you know the people of El Bethel would have helped you every step of the way with the service? That's tradition. That's what she wanted."

Mattie cleared her throat and approached them as Gabrielle stood still.

"Clarence, how are you?" She rubbed his shoulder, ignoring Watford and Amelia.

His face untightened. He took her hands in his. "Ms. Mattie. It's good to see you." He hugged her and pointed to a plush, burgundy pew. Feeling the chill of Mattie's rebuff, Amelia and Watford mingled with other guests.

Nestled on the pew, Clarence took a few deep breaths and fixed his gaze on Mattie.

"I wish someone had let me know about Emma sooner. I came when I could, but I know I should have done more for my sister."

"New York isn't next door."

"Planes and trains roll out every day."

"She told me about your circumstances. Shoot, three times a year is more than a lot of visits most of us get at Grand Oak."

Clarence twiddled with the hymnal in the pew's slot. "Dialysis made it hard for me to travel, but I loved my sister so much, Ms. Mattie."

"I know you did, Son. I know you did."

"We were the last living siblings. It's just me now. Emma practically raised me after Momma, Daddy, and Vernita died. I tried to get closer to her after we were grown, but Watford and Amelia sucked the life out of her. Always wanting and needing, never giving back."

Mattie gave him a knowing nod, familiar with the parasitic nature of family. She pulled the slip of paper from her purse and handed it to Clarence.

"These are Emma's handwritten funeral plans." She also removed a small manila envelope. "These are also some letters she wrote before she got sick. I came in here to ask her children what happened with the order of service and pass the letters along, but you lit into them better than I could."

Clarence's eyes welled up at the sight of his sister's writing. Until a year ago when her health deteriorated, she sent him handwritten letters telling him of her adventures with Mattie. Emma drew a heart on the end of her A's. He tucked the letters in his breast pocket.

"When do you leave for New York?"

"Next Thursday. We meet with the attorney next Tuesday for the will reading."

"Clarence, I doubt they're coming to get Emma's things. If you can stop by Monday or Wednesday, I'll have everything ready. Karen will help me pack it up. Emma left behind photo albums, quilts, books, and clothes. She wanted the clothes to go to Goodwill, but if there's something you want to keep, I'm sure she wouldn't mind."

"I'll make sure to stop by."

Gabrielle inched closer to the pew and tapped her mother's shoulder. "Mama, we have to go. We need to get a bite to eat and get you back to Grand Oak," she said softly as she smiled at Clarence.

4
Too Modern For My Tastes

Joshua paused before turning the key to his front door. After a long day at work, his resolve to discuss things with Marilyn tonight strengthened. *Now or never*, he repeated. He'd spoken with her briefly during his lunch break. The moment he told her he had an important announcement to make, she yelped like a puppy and vowed to leave work two hours early. As he entered the foyer, he smelled Marilyn's good home-cooking, saw the extra effort she'd put into the night. Candles flickered throughout the living and dining rooms as well as the mellow sounds of Boney James ripping his saxophone. He caught a glimpse of Marilyn in the kitchen tossing salad with her favorite tong set. She spun around from her duty, smiled, and met him with a warm hug.

"Baby, I couldn't wait for you to get here!" she said. She released her apron strings, revealing a black, form-fitting dress that hugged her curves in the right places. She'd fashioned her long hair in a bun with a few tendrils hanging. "Let me take your bag, and you have a seat in the living room."

"Mare—"

"No protesting. Sit."

As she returned to the kitchen, he sank into the sofa with a measure of relief and grief tangling inside him. She sashayed toward him with a glass of wine and a small tray of cheese and crackers and scooted next to him, kicking her black designer shoes in the corner.

"My dogs are barking for dear life." Her soft, dark eyes and warm smile had a hypnotic effect on him. She caressed his face and planted another gentle kiss on his cheek.

"What's with the romantic setting?" He sipped the full-bodied red wine, happy she'd listened to his request to toss the sweet wines she adored.

She swigged her wine as her hands trembled. "This doesn't happen every night. I want everything to be special before our discussion," she said, winking and taking another gulp of her wine.

"Marilyn, I—"

"Uh-uh. No talking until after dinner."

Marilyn loosened Joshua's tie, took him by the hand, and led him to the dining room table. She knew her way around the kitchen, and she'd knocked herself out tonight. Joshua's stomach growled as he looked at the spread on the table. She'd prepared his favorite dishes: seafood stuffed grilled salmon, steamed asparagus, tossed salad, and homemade French bread. Two covered dessert plates caught his attention. He knew her sweet potato cheesecake was nestled beneath them. They sat, and he said grace.

Joshua loved the beautiful woman before him. When they'd met nine months ago by happenstance at a bar, they'd both been stood up by blind dates. Once they established she wasn't Vivian and he wasn't Hector, they chuckled and struck up a lively conversation. Drinks turned into a dinner date, walks in the park, and occasional trips out of town. When Gigi met Marilyn for the first time, she blurted, "What happened to Jamie?" *Marilyn happened to Jamie*, he wanted to say, but coughed and ignored the question. His mother called him the runaway groom, accused him of being commitment phobic. He loved the company of ladies, but only one woman captured his heart and her whereabouts were unknown. There was no shortage of women in Savannah. Good women, too. Independent with their own houses, cars, jobs, anything a man like him desired. He wondered if those same women would give him a chance if he didn't make a good living as an engineer, had a house, and didn't require they drop him off at work or loan him a little something when he was light. Marilyn Tharp, Dr. Marilyn Tharp, was successful in her own right as a chemist and researcher with Procter and Gamble in Albany, Georgia, when she shucked off the corporate title and joined the faculty of Savannah State University. He'd enjoyed attending faculty functions with her, and getting to know her colleagues, but still…

"So there's no escaping his visit next summer," she said, breaking his errant thoughts.

"What did you say, Marilyn?"

"I said, my brother wants to come visit us next summer, and I wasn't sure if you'd be okay with him staying with us."

"Whoa, what about your house, Mare?"

"It will be on the market in two weeks."

She took another swig of her drink, stood and approached him. She raised the covered dessert plate next to him and placed a black, velvety box in her hand. She dropped to one knee, scaring Joshua. The platinum and diamond band sparkled in the candlelight. His objection was too slow; she spoke before he could stop her.

"Joshua Marcus Benson, you are the best man I've ever met. You are all I've dreamed of, fantasized about, and craved since I was a little girl. You're strong, loving, independent, and handsome enough to make the cutest babies in Savannah. Will you marry me?"

Joshua shook his hands vigorously. "No, no, no, Mare. Not this."

She stood. "You said you had an announcement to make. I figured we were on the same page, so I decided to beat you to the punch. You hadn't planned on proposing to me tonight?"

Joshua sighed. Four engagements had taught him not to hint at marriage if he wasn't sure. He'd never given her any indication he wanted to marry. They'd dated, had fun, but he never mentioned commitment. He'd also bought rings for his women. It shouldn't be the other way around.

"I wanted to talk to you about my mother."

"Your mother?"

"Let's sit down in the living room and discuss this." He gently caressed Marilyn's arm, but she snatched it away.

"We can stand here and talk."

Joshua sat at the table and pointed to Marilyn's vacant seat; she followed suit. They were adults, and blaring police lights didn't belong in his quiet neighborhood. "I came home to ask for my key back and for you to move your things. I've rearranged my schedule to work from home, and I'm moving my mother in with me. I've hired a homecare health aide, and I plan to surprise her with this news at the Grand Oak Christmas Pageant."

"Are you telling me I sat here and made a fool of myself, cooking for you, spending time with you, and you don't even want to be with me?"

"Marilyn, I said nothing about ending the relationship. I'm freeing my house for my mom. My sisters aren't willing to take her in, so I'm doing what I have to do for my mother. She's miserable at that place. I can't believe Gigi put her there."

"I can help with your mother."

"Come on, Marilyn, it was obvious she annoyed you when she was here."

"She peed in the bed."

"She's elderly, Mare."

"She insulted my cooking."

"Her dietary needs have changed over the years, Mare. She can't eat spicy or salty foods without upsetting her stomach. You made her enchiladas and filled them with jalapeño peppers." He paused, then took a deep breath. "Our parents sacrificed so much for us, and it's time for me to give back."

"Give back all you want! Best believe it will be without me." Marilyn jumped from her seat, knocking it to the floor. She grabbed the ring box and marched toward the stairs.

"Mare, don't do this."

She continued her brisk stride as he followed her. She headed toward the guest bedroom where she'd put a few items in the closet. It made sense to bring clothes and leave them here when she spent the night. His house was closer to Savannah State than hers, and he said he didn't mind. *If he didn't want me, he shouldn't have led me on*, she muttered as she plucked her business suits from hangers. Angrier now, she voiced her ire with each yank.

"I'm not getting back out here on this dating scene with these non-working, trifling men."

She stuffed clothes in a box she found in the bottom of the closet.

"Always trying to move in on you when you're not looking."

Camisoles.

"Wanting to have a baby and can't take care of themselves."

Stilettos.

"Don't know a salad fork from a dinner fork."

Two coats.

Joshua stood in the doorway watching her. He loved her, but he wasn't ready to take the next step. He approached her gingerly, wanting to assist with the clothes and calm her.

"Let me help."

"You've done enough!"

In one swoop, she raked jewelry on the dresser into the box.

"Mare, calm down."

She faced him. "This is the last time I'm asking. Will you marry me?"

He saw the love and sincerity in her eyes, but wouldn't yield. "Marilyn, I can't."

She hoisted the box from the side of the dresser where she dropped in the last pair of earrings. "You had your chance. After tonight, don't call me, don't email me, don't get in touch with me. I'm thirty-seven years old with a time clock ticking louder than Big Ben. I've wasted almost a year with someone who doesn't even think I'm worthy to be his wife."

"Marilyn, proposing to a man is too modern for my tastes. If you'd be patient, we can continue our relationship to see where it goes."

Marilyn's steely look chilled Joshua. Marilyn spat in her hand and slapped Joshua so hard his face burned.

"Fuck you, Joshua Benson. Fuck you!"

5
Husband First–Always

"We don't need organized religion to be connected to God."

"Hallowed Beryl, we should call the authorities. We could get some of the—"

"Are you raising your voice at me?"

"No, I only meant—"

"That's what I thought. I'm still the head of this household. Don't you *ever* forget your place!"

Alice nodded in deference to her husband, glued to the spot where the berating began. As Beryl's chest rose and fell, she attempted to suppress his anger with, "your dinner is getting cold. You need to come eat."

"Warm it up for me."

Alice headed to the kitchen and took Beryl's plate from the table. Though they owned a microwave, she was forbidden to warm his food in it. After their short-lived membership with the Friends of Sinai, Beryl mistrusted microwaves, said they were another way the world conspired to fill bodies with toxins and cancer. He believed food was best warmed in the oven, covered with foil and heated through, or reheated on top of the stove, covered in foil, over a pan of boiling water. He demanded his non-alcoholic drinks have seven ice cubes, because seven was the biblical number of completion. Alice rarely used the icemaker; Beryl stood over her as she filled the old-fashioned ice cube trays to assure she manually released them in his glass. She pressed the preheat button on the oven to 325 degrees and stood against the island. They adhered to a strict bedtime of nine o'clock, so she had less than an hour to heat the food, wash the dishes, and take a shower. She removed two juicy ribeye steaks from his plate with tongs—Beryl said meat lost its flavor if pierced with a fork—and laid them side-by-side. She covered his jumbo baked potato with fresh foil. Joshua had called her two days ago with news of Emma Jelks's passing and funeral arrangements. The few times she interacted with Ms. Emma in her mother's room, she was grateful for the friendship that developed between the ladies. When she asked if she could attend the funeral, Beryl only stared. She wanted to confide in someone about her feelings, but she didn't feel comfortable speaking the truth. No one knew the emotions growing inside her, not even her acquaintance, Synaria, from the library. She massaged her temples and played the feelings in her head like a short film. The longing for her parents, Gabrielle, and Joshua grew stronger each day. She missed the laughter they shared, even the bickering. She missed her parents' Jesus and the Sunday morning pilings into their Chrysler minivan. Joshua kicked off the backseat singing with "Jesus Loves Me." Both laughed at Gabrielle's tone deafness, but she didn't care. They sang at the top of their lungs as Mattie and Daniel beamed with pride. Daniel always nudged Mattie's knee and said, "We're training them up the right way."

Mattie smiled and retorted, "They'd better not depart from it."

Alice jumped when the timer beeped. She slid the food in the oven on a cookie sheet and closed the door. In the thirteen years she'd been married, their latest crisis made her contemplate something she never imagined: divorce. The Bensons were not divorcing people. Daniel made her promise him to keep their marriage Christ-centered and seek counseling if things got rocky. The agreement went well when they were Christians; now she wasn't sure what she was. Or what they were. She looked down at one of the six frumpy dresses she'd purchased from Goodwill; she was grateful Beryl had given her fifty dollars from her paycheck; her normal weekly allowance was thirty dollars. She didn't make as much money at the library as she did with the government job she held when they first married, but during their short stint with the International House of Praise, the elders of the church convinced Beryl a wife's place was in the home; only part-time jobs were allowed. She didn't seek full-time employment after getting a floater position at the library. Like clockwork, he picked her up from the Bull Street branch on Fridays, drove to Chatham County Federal Credit Union, and pulled into the first parking space closest to the door. Alice signed the back of her check and turned it over to Beryl because he spurned the notion of direct deposit. They strolled up to Shelby's window, the teller most familiar with them. He asked for thirty dollars and handed it to Alice. The rest was deposited into an account with his name only. Same thing. Every Friday.

"I don't have all night to eat! I'm hungry."

Alice blinked back tears. "It should be warm enough," she called into the living room.

His movement was swift as he entered the kitchen. "You know better than to address me that way! Try it again."

Alice watched her husband walk away. Ten years her senior, he was one of the most eligible bachelors in Savannah when they married. Although he worked by day in management at Georgia Pacific Savannah River Site, he was known throughout the region for his business, Parker Trolleys. Beryl Parker supplied transportation to Savannah's booming tourism industry. Gone was the tall, robust man who women gave triple-takes when they dated. His back bent a bit, his warm, dark eyes lost the sparkle they once held, and his love for jazz, restaurants, and sex diminished with each church they joined. The crisis they faced left his eyes rheumy and his gait slower. He was too young to be so sullen. She exhaled and walked in the living room.

"Hallowed Beryl, your food is ready."

She walked five paces ahead of him, taking care to reach the dining room table before he entered the room. She pulled his chair back, waited for him to be seated, and gently placed a napkin across his lap. She joined him, taking a seat to his right.

Clanking silverware was their conversation. Beryl devoured the meal, dousing his steak with A-1 and heaping his potato with butter, sour cream, and bacon.

"Hallowed—"

"Don't start."

"It's not about the situation."

"Good." He chewed, considered the glower on Alice's face. "What is it, then?"

"Well, we were all invited to the Christmas pageant at Grand Oak. I didn't commit to Mama, but it would be so nice to go. The food, Christmas carols, it would be like old times."

"Old times for whom? We don't participate in those affairs."

"What's the harm?"

"I said no."

Mattie's face flashed in Alice's mind. An uncharacteristic surge of courage coursed through her veins and danced on her tongue. "Have you ever thought of what your life would be like without me?"

Beryl took a long swig of lemonade. "My Smith and Wesson holds enough bullets to help anyone rest easy. Always has, always will."

The threat made Alice shiver.

To solidify his point, Beryl offered, "Where would you go? What would you do? Selfish Gigi doesn't even let you all in the house. You'd have to move out Joshua's women to stay at his house. All it takes is for me to make a few phone calls and you couldn't rent an apartment, buy a house, or secure a divorce lawyer in this town."

Her shoulders slumped. She wished she could summon the moxie of the old Alice, the one who shopped, loved clubs, and defended herself against anyone who disrespected her.

"Did you hear me? You're not going anywhere."

"Yes, Hallowed."

"And another thing." Beryl pointed his steak sauce-filled fork toward Alice's face and waited for her to repeat the mantra.

"Husband first. Always."

6
Nowhere To Be Found

Karen tried to lift Mattie's funk with no luck. She had smuggled Mattie's favorite peaches from the cafeteria along with three cinnamon packets. The cups of untouched peaches sat on the table, along with a warm cup of cranberry ginger ale. Karen sat next to Mattie on the bed.

"Ms. Mattie, is everything okay?"

"Not right now, but it will be."

"Is it about Ms. Emma?"

Mattie shook her head. "I'm not sad. I'm happier than I've been in a long time."

"You sure could've fooled me. Looking lost and sad. This is not my Mattie."

"If you want your Mattie, loosen up my curls some. I asked Kennedy to keep them tight for the pageant tonight. I want to look good when I join in the songs."

Karen removed the scarf from Mattie's head. She found her favorite plastic pick in the top drawer and gently fluffed out her curls. Mattie took great pride in her appearance; her hair was thicker than a lot of the women at Grand Oak. Some of them envied Mattie because she didn't wear a wig.

"Am I loosening your curls for singing, or Mr. Kauthon?"

"Who?"

"Don't act like you can't tell he's sweet on you."

"Kauthon is my TV buddy, nothing more, nothing less. He's a good guy and tells a lot of funny jokes. As innocent as he looks, he tells dirty jokes sometimes, too. He's just a friend to pass the time away."

"Mmm-hmmm, Ms. Mattie."

"He is. Agatha is the one who's sweet on him, but he said she gossips too much. He needs a more discreet lady friend. You know Grand Oak is nothing but a little Peyton Place."

"Peyton Place?"

Mattie looked at Karen. "It was a book and a TV show, but when people use the phrase they mean a place where a lot of messiness happens." Mattie touched Karen's hand as she picked her hair. "See, I didn't make you Google it."

They laughed so hard they didn't see Kauthon standing in the doorway or hear him clearing his throat.

"Guess Comedy Central is in Room 187."

Karen's head jerked at the sound of his voice. She motioned him to come in and pointed at the empty seat next to Mattie's bed. "Mr. Kauthon, Ms. Mattie was just telling me about an old TV show, *Peyton Place.*"

Kauthon smiled and nodded. "Went downhill after Mia Farrow left. Even had Ruby Dee on there. You know it was good to see some of us on prime time." He leaned back in his seat, pining for his younger days.

"How do you know all that about a show? Weren't you working?" Mattie semi-glanced at him, careful not to disrupt Karen's work. She'd never tell him how handsome he was. His gray suit fit him just right, and the blue-and-gray tie he wore accented his attire perfectly. His clean-shaven face and bald head lopped years off his appearance. The gleaming, silver hoop in his left ear was the only thing Mattie didn't like. Agatha and the other women called him Harry Belafonte. She agreed with their comparison.

"I worked, but my wife loved the show. Talked about the cast like they were old friends. She gardened, sewed, cooked, and loved her soaps."

"I see," said Mattie.

"After the war, I worked the highway, then the saw mill. I provided for my wife and daughter."

Done with her task, Karen said, "Ms. Mattie, I have to go to Doc Jamison's room. Bed pan changes."

Mattie held her arm. "Don't go."

"Duty calls." Karen gave her a sly smile and left the room.

Kauthon scooted close to Mattie. "You scared to be alone with me?" He chuckled and moved back, not wanting to make her uncomfortable.

"Kauthon Spence, I am no such a thing. I will pop you in the head with my cane if you bother me."

"A woman with a little fight in her. I like that."

"You need to worry about Agatha. If she comes by here and sees you, she'll get jealous and accuse us of doing something."

"Agatha's what all the other women in here are to me. A friend."

"Suit yourself."

"She's no Ruby Dee."

"What's Ruby Dee got to do with our conversation?"

Kauthon laid his hand over his heart before he shared his secret. "Ruby Dee used to make my nature rise."

Mattie covered her ears. "I don't want to hear about your nature. It's probably gone."

"Don't you believe I'm natureless for a minute."

"You men are something else. You know that Viagra will give you a heart attack."

"Everybody has to die from something." He leaned forward in the chair, his expression more serious this time. "I came down to tell you goodbye."

Shocked, Mattie waited for an explanation.

"My daughter, Francine, is coming from Connecticut tomorrow to pick me up. She spent the last year getting things together financially so she could take care of me. Even quit her job two weeks ago. She's good with money, though, like my late wife was."

"Oh."

Kauthon took Mattie's hand. "You seem upset. Did I say something wrong?"

"Seems like everybody's leaving. Emma. Now you."

He caressed her hand. "I was coming by to ask if I could write you sometimes. I'll miss my Southern buddies, but I want to keep in touch. You made my days here a little easier, and I'm grateful to you."

She blushed, unaccustomed to the heat flushing her face. She hadn't felt such heat since menopause, and that was eons ago. "Well, glad I could help."

"Really, Mattie, I've watched you endure your children's absence. Your son seems to be the one who comes most often."

She faced the window. "I bet you all talk about me behind my back, don't you?"

"No. Hell, most of us may as well be toys in misfit land. A weak bladder, expensive medication, and a little forgetfulness, and we get tossed in here. Most of us, anyway. I know I'm blessed to have my daughter looking after me, but I know everybody's not so lucky."

"My time's almost up here too," she muttered.

"Beg your pardon?"

"Nothing." Mattie opened a bottom drawer and retrieved her purse. "Will you do me a favor?"

"Sure."

Mattie gave Kauthon her phone. "Call my children to see if they're coming to the pageant tonight."

"Why don't—" He amended his question. "What are their names? I know your son is Joshua, but I get your daughters' names mixed up."

"Gabrielle and Alice. Scroll down the contacts to the first letters. I called the girls earlier in the week with no luck. Joshua said he was coming, though. It's close to start time and they haven't made it."

He spied her message icon. "You have a text message."

"Open it."

He manipulated the device in his large hands and read, *"Running behind but have a big surprise for you. Love you. Josh."*

She beamed. "I pray he's here soon. They all need to get here soon."

He left voice messages for Gabrielle and Alice. "You think they'll find it odd hearing a man's voice?"

"They know I can't stand that cell phone. Karen leaves messages for me all the time. I use my phone every blue moon."

He stood. "Let's head on down to the rec room. I want a good seat."

They headed to the recreation room, moseying past Agatha who stood outside her door. She smirked but didn't speak.

Kauthon grabbed Mattie's hand; she welcomed the gesture by gripping his hand tighter. Her children were nowhere to be found, but her friend was near. That was good enough for her.

7
Here But I'm Gone

Mattie half-watched the children's interpretive dance. Outfitted in sparkling red leotards, red stockings, and green tutus, five girls pranced around the rec room in sync, lifting their hands and moving to the rhythm of a familiar gospel song. Mattie eyed the door. In the fantasy she'd entertained since being seated, Joshua, Alice, and Gabrielle would slip in, take a seat next to her, and enjoy the scene. Kauthon, swept up in the performance, lifted hands in praise to the words being sung, oblivious to her wringing hands. Around the room sat mothers with sons and daughters, aunts, and uncles, enjoying the program and each other. Some of her hall mates were without relatives, but many were joined by their "adopted" kin, young men and women who volunteered at Grand Oak and visited the residents frequently. She'd eyed the door so long, she didn't realize the dance was over. Applause broke the trance the door held over her.

"Weren't the Honeysuckle Dancers marvelous?" said Nancy Ford. Each year the pageant was grander than the last. Nancy took pride in her title as activities director, and this year was the best yet.

Nancy also took the Ugly Sweater Contest too seriously. This year's getup was a red sweater dress with gold tassels around the collar and hem, and a 3-D Santa sewn in the middle of the dress with blinking lights in garland encircling his fat frame. Nancy had taken care to wear makeup and style her hair, usually kept in two flowing braids. The microphone stand had been adjusted earlier to accommodate her petite stature. She stood behind the stand and swabbed her face with a pink handkerchief.

"This is by far the hardest part of the service. Grand Oak Acres is a family, and when we lose a family member, we lose a link in our sturdy chain."

Residents nodded. A round of whispers arose as volunteers took their place behind a decorated oblong table. Mattie counted the unlit candles on the table, eighteen in all. Soft music flowed from a mounted projector as the words *In Memory* flashed across the screen amid a background of white Calla Lilies. She'd forgotten about the *In Memory* phase of the program. Emma's voice rang out in her ear: "they'd better not put no ugly picture of me on that screen." Her throat caught as she shook Emma's voice away. This would be the first year she sat through the ceremony without her crony.

Nancy recited their names alphabetically as a candle was lit for each person. Kauthon held her hand when Emma's face emerged. A Gullah Festival photo depicting Emma dancing with a blue ball of cotton candy had been chosen. She leaned over to Kauthon. "Excuse me, please."

She gathered her purse and went to the bathroom. She stared at herself in the mirror, Emma's image renewing her sense of urgency. Grand Oak had been good to her, better than two of her three children, but it wasn't home. She took a few deep breaths, pulled her phone from her purse, and dialed Gabrielle first.

"Gigi, the program is ending soon. Please come join me. I hoped you talked to Alice and Joshua about the rotation. I want to come home again."

She ended the call and dialed Alice's home number. Beryl had forbidden her to have a cell phone. He'd found the one she'd purchased for Alice and handed it to the trash men on pick-up day. The phone and a few other offenses caused Beryl to toss her from their home. The phone rang three times before Beryl, groggy with an edge of anger in his tone, answered, "Parker residence. How may I help you?"

"It's Ms. Mattie, Beryl. May I please speak to Alice?"

"She's in bed. I'll have her call you tomorrow."

"It's really important. I need to tell her something."

"Ms. Mattie, her bedtime is at nine. She has work in the morning and I refuse to disturb her."

She ended the call without saying goodbye. She knew Joshua would be there; probably too late. She checked her voicemails in anticipation of hearing her children's voices. Joshua's text message helped, but it wasn't his voice. She rubbed the back of her neck and rejoined Kauthon in the rec room.

"I was about to come after you. I figured the tribute would be hard on you."

"Since Emma passed, I feel like I'm here, but I'm gone."

"Time'll heal it."

"Who said I had a lot of time left?"

"Don't say that."

"That's easy for you to say. Come tomorrow you'll be in Connecticut with your daughter. It's almost Christmas and my children haven't brought me anything, not even a fruitcake."

Kauthon chuckled, asked her, "Do you really want one?"

They both laughed. They watched as the El Bethel Senior Choir assembled their instruments. The troop closed out the program every year with special requests from the residents. She scribbled "Carol of The Bells" on one of the request slips Nancy distributed two weeks ago. Daniel played a stirring rendition of the song every Christmas until arthritis wouldn't allow him. She glanced at her watch again and settled back in her seat. Kauthon swayed to the songs, his feet tapping with the drummer's rhythm. When the last song ended, everyone stood to their feet with thunderous applause.

Nancy stood behind the microphone stand again, her shoulders moving to the instrumental accompaniment from the band. "This concludes our pageant for the year. El Bethel's Senior Choir outdid themselves this year." She turned sideways and pointed at them as each member nodded with glee at the acknowledgment. "Please fellowship with them and enjoy the refreshments we've provided."

Kauthon rose, stretched, and shook his pant legs free. "I'm not much for all this mingling. I need my traveling rest." He extended his left hand and helped Mattie to her feet. "I'll walk you back to your room."

She stood as well but swatted his hand. "I *am* in a mingling mood. I plan to stick around a little while longer. You go on back to your room. I'll swing by there when I'm done."

He tipped his hat to her and gently kneaded her shoulder. "I had a really good time."

After he reached the door, Mattie uttered under her breath, "maybe in another lifetime." As he walked away, her heartrate quickened as she touched her right wrist. *Shackle free.* Cathy's Famous Punch was calling her name. She approached the refreshment table as Agatha chatted with Corneila and Harriet.

"They sang better this year. I know it was because of the tenor up front," said Agatha. She pulled her mink stole closer and winked at him.

Corneila and Harriet exchanged glances.

"Didn't you notice how he looked at me?"

"I didn't notice," said Harriet, daintily adding finger sandwiches and fruit to her plate.

"Well, he did. I don't see a ring on his finger, either. Maybe he's a widower."

Mattie couldn't resist the urge to stir the gossip pot. She ladled punch and said, "He'd probably be perfect for you now that Kauthon's leaving."

"Leaving?" Corneila, Harriet, and Agatha spoke in unison.

Mattie sipped. Waited. "He didn't tell you he's moving to Connecticut?"

Agatha's face dropped at the news. "He hasn't said anything to me. I at least want to say goodbye to him. I wanted to get to know him better and now he's leaving."

"He's gone to bed now and you know he can sleep through a hurricane. I wouldn't disturb him if I were you."

Everyone knew Agatha had crept into Kauthon's room in the middle of the night at least three times. He began locking his door the night he woke up and discovered her next to him wearing lingerie and a chin-length bob wig. The street committee said he told her, "This ain't Halloween and I don't feel like playing tricks with you. Go back to your room, Agatha!"

Agatha redirected her focus on Tenor Man. She walked away from them and chatted up the older man as he helped the band members pack their instruments.

"Agatha is too old to be carrying on like some teenager," said Corneila.

"There's a difference between spunk and desperation. She thinks she has spunk, but God knows it's desperation," said Harriet.

Band members stacked instruments on the rec room dolly and walked past the ladies. Mattie yawned. "I'm hitting the sack, too. I'll see y'all in the morning."

She followed closely behind the men, falling in stride with the chatty bass player.

"You fellas need some help?"

"We're just pulling the van around to put the instruments inside."

"Ah, the least you can do is let me hold the door for you," she said, rubbing her right wrist again. Washed in relief about the receptionist's absence, she relaxed and quickened her pace.

She pulled her purse and coat tighter, exiting Grand Oak with the band members. She scanned the parking lot, scared and excited when she saw the familiar car idling on the grass. She ran toward the vehicle, opened the door, and slammed it.

"Drive. Go!" she shouted.

"Ten more minutes and I was about to drive off."

Mattie slid further in her seat as Joshua's SUV turned into the parking lot.

I knew he'd be too late.

8
About What I Said

Colton enjoyed Gabrielle's soft hands on his fleshy back. No other woman, not even his wife, popped the blackheads on his back like she did. In fact, his wife refused to do so. They'd just had a marathon love-making session when he promptly fell asleep. Gabrielle always knocked him out after the first two rounds. A light tap on his shoulder and the whisper, "turn over," roused him from his nap. She'd soaked a face cloth in the bathroom with hot water, straddled his back, and placed it on blackheads that had sprung up like weeds. She insisted they stay at the Mansion on Forsyth Park tonight. She mentioned going to Grand Oak to see her mother, but they got bogged down doing their business. He planned to break the news to her the moment they got to the room, but one thing led to another, and they were locked in heated passion. Now her yammering sounded like Charlie Brown's teacher. Roselle expected him home in two hours, and he hadn't planned on disappointing her. She nuzzled his ears as he sought the right words.

"...so we could renovate your house, I could sell my house, that way I won't have to live in the house your wife created. I mean, it would be the same structure, but I'd be putting my stamp on it."

"Mmm-hmmm."

"Then we could change church membership, because there is no way I could face those hyenas at Christ Missionary, you being a deacon and all."

"Mmm-hmmm."

Colton's back slackened under the tenderness of her kneading.

"I don't think we should have a big wedding. I'm forty-nine. You're fifty-three. What's somebody gonna give us? A toaster and some Egyptian towels? I think a wishing well would be best."

"Mmm-hmmm."

Gabrielle lightly punched his back. "Say something other than *mmm-hmm*, Colt!"

"That feels good, Gigi."

Something had changed. Colton had been her most generous sponsor. She'd fallen in love with him after six months of dating even though he was married. She remembered him from high school; he was a senior when she entered her freshman year. Strong and muscular, he was the athlete and scholar all the girls wanted. Thirty years later, their paths crossed at Blessingdale's Thrift Shop while Mattie shopped for vintage Club cookware, her retail therapy item of choice. He held a purse and waited in the clothing section of the store. They locked eyes and she immediately recalled the giant, brown-skinned athlete everyone called Doc. She knew he'd chosen academia, walked away from the NFL after reading about him in the *Savannah Tribune*. Gabrielle's jaw dropped when his wife exited the dressing room. She was bigger than a Hollywood mansion. Water rolled down her three chins as she modeled the too-tight evening gown for Colton. She did a double-take, recognized the woman was his high school sweetheart and head cheerleader, Roselle Jones. Gone was the brick house all the young men admired. Gabrielle sauntered over to them in a tight yellow blouse and fitted jeans. She gripped her designer purse and asked, "Aren't you Doc and Roselle?" She adjusted her sunglasses above her forehead.

She saw the lust in his eyes and embarrassment in Roselle's face as she sucked in her gut. Roselle gave her the head-to-toe once-over and dropped her head.

"Do I know you?" he asked, taking the lead and approached her.

"I was a few years behind you guys. Gabrielle Benson." She shook his hand.

"Oh. I remember you." He turned to Roselle. "Rose, you remember Gabrielle. I think you all mentored the younger girls during cheerleading summer camp."

"You look familiar." Roselle mopped sweat from her face with a small cloth draped across her shoulder. "Time's been good to you."

"You as well," Gabrielle lied.

After an awkward pause, Gabrielle pointed at Mattie. "I have to get back to Mama. She's going to buy out all of Savannah's cooking pots if I don't get to her. It was nice seeing you two again."

"It was nice to see you also," he said.

She walked away knowing something unspoken hung in the air between them. She was done with Johnny, her last sponsor, and wanted someone new to explore. She also wanted to finally settle down, stop playing games.

She rubbed Colton's back softer as his words came rushing back to her. *You're so beautiful. Roselle let herself go a long time ago. You're the kind of woman I want for my wife. You look good and you take care of yourself.*

"When we first got here, you said you wanted to tell me something," she said, rubbing warmed jojoba oil on his back. She licked his inner ear and the side of his face.

He shook his head. "That drives me crazy. Stop."

She chuckled. She'd learned his hot spots early on and used them to her financial advantage.

"Let me turn over. I have to say this face to face. It's about what I said. About us being together, I mean."

He grabbed the remote and turned on the television.

"This sounds important. I don't want a television playing," she said.

"I need some background noise."

"Colt, why?"

"I'm nervous."

"Let's compromise. I'll mute it for now." She silenced the chatter. "Satisfied?" she asked, anticipating his proposal.

He sat up in his boxers and rubbed her face. His back to the TV, he took a deep breath. "Gigi, reconnecting with you has been indescribable. It's been a long time since I've laughed this much, traveled, talked about my feelings, aspirations."

She rubbed his hands, loving the prospect of not being single and fifty.

"I do, however, need to apologize. What we've been doing is wrong and I feel horrible. You see—"

Her hyperventilating scared him. Gabrielle placed her hand over her chest, gasping for air. He hadn't broken the worst of the news and she was a mess. He didn't know she was so fragile. He tried a different approach.

"I know you feel I led you on, but—"

This time she screamed, pointed to the television. His eyes widened as he watched the breaking news story. He pressed the mute button on the remote, watched her mother's face on the screen. The newscaster reported in a grim voice, "A Mattie's Call has been issued for Grand Oak resident, Mattie Benson. She is a seventy-two-year-old African American woman, five feet seven inches tall with shoulder-length auburn hair. She was last seen wearing a gray sweater, black slacks, and a black wool peacoat. If you know of her whereabouts, please contact the Savannah Police Department immediately."

9
Upped And Walked Away?

Gabrielle watched Colton speed away after dropping her off at the Grand Oak entrance. He said they'd pick up the conversation later, but she didn't care. Guilt wracked her body as she trudged down the hill to the facility and watched the activity going on outside. Police cars and an ambulance were posted near the front door. Through the glass door, she saw Joshua in heated conversation with a woman in a business suit and a police officer. Ms. Agatha stood near them as well. She quickened her pace but was stopped by an officer near the door.

"What business do you have here?"

"The missing woman. Mattie Benson. She's my mother."

The officer scanned the names and photos on the checklist he'd been given. "Are you Gabrielle?"

"Yes."

"Right this way."

He escorted her inside. The front lobby, filled with residents and staff, oozed the familiar antiseptic and applesauce scents Gabrielle had come to despise. Joshua's voice spat thunder to the nursing home administrator and a police officer as everyone kept their distance.

"So you're telling me, with all these damn security cameras in this building, you didn't see my seventy-plus-year-old mother walk away?" He pointed to the overhead cameras for emphasis. "A seventy-plus-year old woman upped and walked away and no one saw anything?"

"Sir, we're trying to get to the bottom of this matter. She must have left after the pageant."

Gabrielle moved closer, touched Joshua's shoulder. A slight bit of relief covered his face when he saw her.

"Gigi, this woman is saying she doesn't know how Mama walked away!"

"Josh, calm down. We won't solve anything with you screaming."

He turned his venom on her. "Maybe if you had been screaming, or caring, or at least been here for the pageant like she asked you and Alice, she wouldn't be missing. Would she?"

"Doesn't look like you were here either!"

"I texted her. She knew I was running late."

The scent of sex with Colton rose in her nostrils and she averted her brother's cold gaze. She was laid up with someone's husband, and all her mother wanted was a little bit of her time. She looked around. "Where is Alice anyway?"

"Probably in bed asleep next to that monster she calls a husband. I called three times and nobody answered."

"Let's take this into Mrs. Ross's office," the officer suggested.

They followed her into the office with Agatha in tow. The men allowed the ladies to have a seat. Marci Ross kept a fresh pot of coffee brewing in her office, and she offered everyone a cup. Joshua breathed heavy and directed his questions to Agatha.

"Tell me what happened again."

"We were at the Christmas pageant at the rec room. Your mother had walked down with Kauthon Spence, then he left. The band from the church was the last group to perform. After they packed up everything, I saw your mother walk out with the band. I figured she was going back to her room."

"What about the security system?" he asked.

Marci fidgeted. "Mr. Benson, your mother's Wander Guard

bracelet malfunctioned two days ago. It worked better on her left arm, but she insisted her left arm was for the watch your father gave her, so she wore it on the right. It was being serviced and should have been returned yesterday. The repair was delayed, so that's how she was able to walk out undetected. If she'd worn the bracelet, the alarm would have triggered the door sensor. We are so sorry. It was a huge mistake on our part."

"No one was at the front desk monitoring anything?" Gabrielle asked.

"Not to my knowledge. The receptionist said she stepped away for a moment to use the bathroom. The other staff were busy helping residents back to their rooms."

"What about Karen, the CNA who's always with Mama?"

"She worked half-day today."

Quelling the growing tension, Officer Jimmerson said, "Rest assured, we will find your mother. The Mattie's Call is being announced throughout the area, so she'll turn up. She couldn't have gotten too far."

"She's lonely and missing Emma. That's all it is. She'll be back," said Agatha. "I told you all what I know. May I please go back to my room now?"

"Of course, Agatha. Thank you," said Marci.

Marci opened her drawer and pulled out a stack of business cards. She jotted her personal cell number on back of two and slid them to Gabrielle and Joshua. "I'm available around the clock. We will do everything we have to do for your mother."

Officer Jimmerson offered his card as well. "I'll be in touch. You have my word."

Marci broke the silence. "There is nothing more we can do right now. Did you two want to go to her room?"

Gabrielle nodded, then held Joshua's hand. "She asked me for jewelry two weeks ago. I want to make sure nothing valuable is taken from her. Josh and I can take some of her things tonight and come back tomorrow."

They walked out of Marci's office and met the pitiful gazes of the residents. A few of them turned away while others approached them.

"They gon' find Ms. Mattie. Watch what I say, here?" said one woman.

"She'll be back in no time," said one of the men.

Gabrielle and Joshua accepted their soft hugs and nodded at their optimism.

"It's bedtime. Let's all get to our rooms," Marci said, as if using a teacher's outside voice.

The siblings, with Marci in tow, took slow strides to their mother's room. When they entered, they smelled Mattie's favorite perfume. At home, she misted the master bedroom with perfume or simmered citrus potpourri. She'd made her bed as she did when they lived at home: neat and quarter bouncing tight. They opened drawers, her closet, and looked under her bed. Save two coats, a half-eaten package of Berry Burst Oreos, and an unopened box of Dixie cups, her belongings were all gone.

10
Don't Question My Authority

"I suggest you tell your mother not to call the house after eight o'clock," Beryl said, parking in front of the library.

Alice concentrated on the shelving carts she'd have to stock, the interlibrary loans she needed to process, and the dream she'd had the night before. In it, time stood still, and on her wedding day, Daniel stood with her in the ladies dressing room. He looked distinguished in his black tuxedo. He told a few jokes, then his countenance became serious. He lifted her veil and said, "I can see farther down the road than you. You don't have to do this if you don't want to, Baby Girl. There'll be other men. There'll be other relationships." She hadn't dreamt of her father since he died; the dream made her feel safe, like Daniel was looking out for her. If the scenario in her dream had happened thirteen years ago, she would have kicked off her pumps, hiked up her wedding dress, and made a beeline for the chapel's gothic front door.

"...that's why I didn't want you to have the cell phone she gave you. She would be calling all times of the day and night." He waited for her response. "Alice, do you hear me talking to you?"

"Hallowed, I want the money back. We need the money back."

"I told you don't ever question my authority!"

Alice held her ground. In her usual meekness, she said, "Hallowed, I know there is more to the story. The truth will come out. It always does."

He yanked her arm as she reached for the door. "You're playing a dangerous game. I don't know what you've done with the Alice I married, but she better be here when I pick you up from work this evening."

"It always does," Alice said, dropping Hallowed and snatching her arm back. She headed into work with her father's voice in her head.

She opened the door and vowed to use the fifteen minutes she had remaining before start time to pull herself together in the ladies room. Tears had flown freely the past three months, something she wasn't accustomed to. Something was dying inside her, and she didn't know what to do. Startled by the presence of her acquaintance, Synaria, Lindsey, the branch manager, and Harvey, another page, she paused.

"What are you doing here?" Synaria asked. "We thought you'd call in."

"I—"

Lindsey walked up to her and placed her arm on her left shoulder. "It's so awful. Your mother was with us three weeks ago doing senior crafts, now this!"

"You all should sue Grand Oak. No way my mother would walk away from a facility and no one could offer an explanation about anything! Anything?" Harvey raised his voice in anger.

The three of them formed a semicircle around her, making her stomach flip.

"What are you all talking about?"

Synaria took the lead. "You don't know what's going on? The Mattie's Call about your mother. You didn't see it?"

Alice's heart raced. They didn't watch TV often in their home. "I went to bed as usual. TVs are evil and no one has called me..." Beryl's words resonated, *Tell your mother not to call the house after eight.* The phone kept ringing last night, and she assumed a bored prankster had too much time on his hands. "Oh God." Alice leaned against the wall as Synaria and Harvey steadied her. Lindsey pressed the automated button for the door.

"Take her in the break room. I'll get some water from the fridge."

Noting her trembling hands and wobbly knees, Harvey picked her up and put her in a chair in the break room. Synaria fanned her face with an *O* magazine left on the table.

Alice struggled to catch her breath but managed to gasp, "When? What..."

"Calm down. You don't need to be here. I can take you home or to relatives, but there's no way you can work with all this going on."

Lindsey wiped the icy water bottle with a napkin and gave it to Alice. She cosigned Synaria's words. "We need to get you back home. I can call in extra help for the next few days, but you should be with family right now."

"Please tell me what happened."

"About ten o'clock last night, there was a television and radio break reporting a missing woman from Grand Oak Acres. When they displayed her face on the screen, I remembered the times you brought her in. She wanted to know why you kept calling me Syn and asked you if I was devilish."

"Where did she go?"

"Not sure. The reporter said she walked out with some people after a Christmas pageant."

Alice winced. Her mother begged her to attend the function and she blew her off.

"Drink the water and breathe. Please." Lindsey disappeared and returned with a bag of yogurt nut mix.

"Who do I need to call for you? Your husband shouldn't have gotten too far. Maybe I can call him and have him come back," said Harvey.

"No!" Alice said, more forceful than she intended. "I mean, he can't leave work."

"What about your brother and sister?" Synaria asked.

Alice's voice lowered almost to a whisper. "I don't know their numbers by heart."

"Are they in your cell phone?"

"I don't have a cell phone."

Synaria kept her poker face intact. She waited as Alice gulped the water, formulating a solution for the crisis. "Tell you what. Let me take you home or I'll drive you to your brother's or sister's place. You all can wait together."

"Let me go home first, then you can take me to Joshua's house. I need to pick up a bank statement and get a few things before Beryl gets home."

Alice grabbed her purse, dizzy and stumbling back a step, grateful for Synaria's generosity but unsure of how to tell her the truth. She was the last person Gigi and Josh wanted to see.

11
Onions And Roses

Synaria played the speech over again in her mind. Ms. Mattie's disappearance wasn't the appropriate segue to broach the subject, but she'd take it. She'd been silent too long and wanted Alice to know she was more than an acquaintance. She was also a friend.

"Are you hungry, Alice?"

"I ate breakfast earlier. I'm surprised I haven't thrown it back up. I'm so worried about Mama."

"I remember where you live. We should be there in no time."

Synaria had never been inside Alice's house. Twice she visited: once to drop off a book, a second time to give Alice two Club Dutch ovens for her mother. Both times her husband met her at the door and wouldn't allow her to speak to Alice. When he dropped her off at work, Synaria stood outside smoking and looking at his wicked frown. Before she'd snuffed out her Virginia Slim, she heard him yell insults at Alice's back and she exited the car. It wasn't until she updated emergency contact information employees that she realized Alice's husband had a real name—Beryl. Her frequent restroom trips, crying spells, and puffy face made Synaria feel helpless. Was it depression, abuse, or both? They were close in age but worlds apart in living conditions. She wanted to get to the bottom of the matter.

"Mind if I ask you something?"

Alice sighed and tinkered with the door handle. "Is it personal?"

"Yes and no. You can tell me it's none of my business and I'll change the subject."

"Ask what you want. I need someone to talk to," Alice said, grateful for the chance to be heard.

She eased into the grilling. "I've been concerned about you lately. Your work hasn't suffered, but it's obvious something is going on."

"My money's gone!" she blurted out.

Synaria glanced at Alice quickly before turning her attention back to the highway. Too many questions would shut her down, and she was proud of the bit of progress they were making.

"Hallowed, I mean, Beryl, did something with our savings." Alice said the words so fast her lips twitched.

"Calm down. Start from the beginning and speak slowly."

"Two years ago, we joined Quest for Excellence Ministries."

"The Ponzi scheme church on the news!" Synaria lowered her volume. "Sorry."

"Hallowed Crenshaw invited a speaker in. He told us he wanted us to be wealthier and enjoy God's fruits. The moment the speaker took to the podium, I had a bad feeling. He told us we'd get a big return on our investments by pooling our money. We'd invest in gentrified areas that were experiencing rapid growth."

"What does Hallowed mean?"

"It is how the men of our church are addressed. At your church the words 'Reverend' or 'Pastor' are probably used. Quest leadership believes men are the heads, the leaders, and should be addressed as such. Women are not allowed to preach there or take the podium in the pulpit either."

"Oh."

"Anyway, I realized a few weeks ago the money I'd squirreled away all these years was gone."

"How did you find out?"

"Hall—" She let out a low cough. "Beryl left a bank statement out. That was my money! Money I brought to the marriage and saved up till now. Gone!" She snapped her finger.

"I read an investigation has been launched against the church. I hope you get a little of the money back."

"I won't. I researched similar schemes on my lunch break last week. Few, if any, parties recoup anything."

"Why do you stay married to Beryl?"

"I don't believe in divorce."

"Do you believe in abuse?"

"Beryl's not abusive. He can be overbearing at times…" Alice heard how pathetic she sounded. She touched Synaria's arm. "Syn, I'm scared."

"What scares you most?"

"Starting over again. I've been isolated so long I don't know what to do."

Synaria pulled into the driveway and kept the engine running. "Get what you need. We'll pick up where we left off when you get back. I'll help you all I can."

Alice fished in her purse for the house key. Their house was one of the few purchases she had a say-so in acquiring. Only Beryl's name was on the property, but she helped with the floor plan and decorated it to her tastes.

She opened the door and stepped inside. She halted after five steps, overwhelmed by the smell of onions and roses. The familiar scent permeated her house. Jazz music thumped throughout the house from surround-sound speakers, her special request when the house was built. She followed the trail of funk up the stairs, stopping at the sound of Beryl's voice.

"That's the way I like it. Don't stop!"

Low moans were the response from his bedmate. Alice gritted her teeth. She kicked the door open, startling Beryl and the woman. She couldn't believe her eyes. Davina Crenshaw. Davina stopped mid-stroke, jumped off Beryl, and fell to the floor. She clutched the mattress, managing to cover herself with the duvet. He pulled the wet sheet around his midsection, raising one arm in surrender.

"Let me explain, Alice!"

"He said you wouldn't sleep with him anymore. I'm so sorry, Alice."

"Shut up, Davina!" he shouted.

Alice picked up the closest object she could find, her favorite decorative ceramic cat, and hurled it at Beryl. The cat shattered against the wall, narrowly missing Davina's head.

"You'd be nasty enough to bring another woman in my house, and you couldn't pick someone clean!"

"It was a mistake, baby. A big mistake!"

Alice turned on her heels, keeping down waves of nausea. She slammed the wall as she hurried downstairs, drowning out Davina's and Beryl's voices following closely behind. When she reached the bottom step, he touched her arm.

"Don't walk out like this. At least hear me out."

She faced them. Davina, now clad in one of Alice's robes, stood next to him. "Please don't tell my husband. If this gets out, the church will be ruined."

"Oh, now you're worried about appearances? You both disgust me."

Davina swept Alice up in a hug. "Sister, God wouldn't be pleased with this dissension."

Overpowered by Davina's body odor mixed with sex, Alice vomited on her. The morning's waffles, eggs, yogurt nut mix, and water cascaded down the robe and Davina's manicured toes. She ran out of the front door, Beryl followed, balancing the sheet wrapped around his body as he yelled, "Don't go, Alice. I'm sorry."

Alice ran toward the car, arms flailing. Synaria opened the door for her as she jumped in. "Go! Get me to Josh's."

"What the hell?"

"I'll explain later."

Synaria backed out the driveway, unsure of how to comfort Alice who was shaking like a caught shoplifter. She opened her mouth to ask what was going on but stopped short when Beryl lost control of the sheet he wore.

I've seen it all. A naked man in December. In Savannah, Georgia.

12
Even As A Child

"Who is it?" Joshua yelled. The banging interrupted the conversation with his boss. Whomever was ringing the doorbell and banging at the same time had better be the police or someone with an update about his mother. "Stu, let me call you back. Some nut is banging on my door."

Joshua took cautious steps to the front door, gazed into the peephole, then relaxed when he saw Synaria. He snatched open the door. "What's wrong? Is Alice okay?"

The look of panic on Synaria's face answered his question. Synaria's shaking head and trembling hands gave him pause.

"Do you need to sit down? Say something, Synaria."

"It's your brother-in-law. He—"

"Did he touch my sister?"

She shook her head. "She caught him with someone in their house and now she's sitting out in my car. She won't talk, she won't move, she won't respond to me at all. She was fine after she got in the car, but she shut down after that and I don't know what to do. She's in a catatonic state."

Joshua stole a glance around Synaria and motioned for her to follow him. They walked to her car, Synaria using the key fob to unlock the door.

Joshua knelt, touched Alice's hair. "Al, it's okay. Whatever happened, it's going to be okay."

Alice stared ahead.

He closed the door and pulled Synaria aside. "Even as a child, Alice couldn't handle conflict or confrontation. Fights on the playground, disagreements with us, disappointment from our parents, and she'd shut down. I'll deal with Beryl later, but right now, you have to help me bring her in."

"What should we do?"

"She can hear us; she won't respond, though. We'll grab either side of her and bring her in the house. My guest bedroom is on the main floor, so the first thing we'll do is get her in there. Open the door for me."

Synaria did as instructed. She gently tugged Alice's right arm and gathered her legs together so she faced the opened door. She pulled her up as Joshua grabbed her left side. They carried her in as Alice faced forward, no expression on her face. They made it to the bed and placed her there. Synaria removed the old coat Alice wore and laid it across a chair. Joshua looked at the homely dress with bits of vomit on the left collar, and unattractive boots his sister wore. Her hair, pulled back in a bun, was streaked with a few strands of gray, no doubt a result of being with that tyrant. When she was herself again, he'd take her shopping and to a beauty salon. One thing he knew: she wouldn't be going back to Beryl.

"Synaria, do you mind getting her out of these shoes and that dirty dress?"

"Not at all."

"I was making lunch. Turkey sandwich and chips okay with you?"

"Sure."

"I'll be back in a few."

Synaria watched him walk away. The other women at the library always made a fuss about Joshua the few times he stopped by to see Alice, but she never paid attention to him. Now she understood why they made a big to-do over him. From his confident swagger, to the low-cut Afro, white teeth, and chiseled body, it was easy to see why women found him sexy. He shared Alice's beautiful, rich brown skin. She turned her attention back to Alice. She soothed her, not waiting for a response.

"Alice, we made it to Joshua's house."

She removed Alice's scuffed boots. The black trouser socks she wore had tiny holes in them.

"I'm taking the rest of the day off and going out to get you a few things. You'd like that, wouldn't you?"

Synaria scanned the bedroom, her eyes settling on a chest-of-drawers in the corner. She took the liberty to inspect the drawers for socks. She pulled out a pair of black socks and found a pair of men's athletic pants and an oversized Savannah State University T-shirt.

"You'll have to help me help you, Sis. We have to get you bathed up and get those teeth brushed."

Synaria's one-sided commentary continued as she found a black paddle brush for Alice's hair.

"The way I see it, everything happens for a reason. What are the odds that I'd take you home and you'd find what you found today? I think I was placed in your path to help you get through this. You'll have to do a lot to get rid of me."

Thankful the bedroom had a bathroom, Synaria turned on the shower. Alice prided herself on cleanliness, and Synaria knew whenever she came to, she'd be furious another woman would let her walk around rancid. That's how she'd justify cleansing her friend.

"Do you have something I can use to transport Alice to the shower?" she called to Joshua.

He padded down the hall to the room. "Mama's wheelchair should be in back of the closet. The shower is accessible also. I had it reconstructed last month. You can wheel her in and sit her in the shower."

"Thanks, Joshua."

Synaria lined up the chair next to the bed. She worked quickly to place Alice in the chair and get her in the bathroom. Alice, loosening up from her experience across town, stared at Synaria.

"What are you doing, Syn?" she asked, barely above a whisper.

"Getting you bathed up. You have vomit on your clothes and you need to brush your teeth. Now that you're responding, I can sit outside and wait until you get yourself cleaned up."

"Don't leave me."

"You need your privacy. I'll be outside the door. I found a T-shirt and jogging pants, but I'm sure you want some feminine clothes to wear. We can go to the mall, or if you tell me what you like, I can get you something. You *won't* be putting that homely dress and shoes back on, though."

Alice shrugged. "Look down in the cabinet and get me the Lever 2000. Mama always brought the soap with her. It was the only kind she wasn't allergic to when she bathed. I like it, too."

Though Alice spoke, Synaria was afraid to leave her alone. She looked around the bathroom as if she'd never visited her brother's house. She scratched at her hair, untangled the bun, and let her hair fall around her face.

"I didn't know you had that much hair."

"Beryl said a woman's hair is her glory and shouldn't be out unless it's a special occasion."

Synaria bit her lip. "Alice, you have a long road ahead of you, but right now, this minute, you can't repeat anything else he said."

"It's second nature."

"A new nature is on the horizon that doesn't include him."

"I have nowhere else to go."

"You have your siblings and you have me. Starting over is not impossible. It's always the first step that's the scariest."

She let the words soak in. Five minutes later, she said, "Let me shower, please."

"Call me if you need me."

Alice tugged Synaria's arm as she walked away. "Thank you."

Synaria nodded. "Anytime."

Alice stood from the wheelchair and moved it aside, memories of Mattie rushing back. She looked at the wheelchair and remembered the last time they were all together was last year, the Fourth of July, on Joshua's deck. Mattie pushed the chair away and danced the Electric Slide. She prepared her famous Italian pasta salad, red velvet cake, and shared stories with them about their childhood. That was the happiest she'd seen her mother in a long time. She felt ashamed that so much time had passed without spending time with her. She looked in the mirror and saw a country bumpkin staring back. Tired eyes, gray hairs, and small lines dancing around the corners of her mouth made her feel older than thirty-eight. Mattie swore by egg-white tighteners and oatmeal honey masks to keep the skin supple. Beryl said aging was a natural process and women who fought it were vain Jezebels. She shook away his voice and turned on the shower. She sat in the corner seat in the shower and let the water run over her. Over the years, she endured criticism from former friends who fell away as she submitted to Beryl. Their voices came back one by one.

"Ain't no way a man would be taking *my* paycheck and giving me my money like I'm some damn child!"

"Husband or not, there woulda been a cast-iron skillet upside his head by now."

"Un-unh, the spirit of Mary Woodson woulda come over me and I'da tossed a pan of hot grits on him."

"We teach men how to treat us, and God knows you oughta love yourself better than that, Alice."

Her tears competed with the water flow rippling overhead. She cried and longed for life as a single woman. She scrubbed harder as Davina Crenshaw's face played over in her mind. Too many years had passed and she didn't know how to start over.

"Something has to give. I'll die if it doesn't."

13
Didn't Look That Way To Me

"So you're telling me that dog didn't have the decency to go to a hotel?" Gabrielle sipped the Mimosa she'd prepared instead of the nonalcoholic drinks Joshua set out for lunch.

"Gigi, I called you over to support our sister, not berate her."

"Josh, I'm not berating her. It's no secret Mama and Daddy didn't want her to marry him. He was too old and too experienced for her."

"Gigi, be quiet!" Synaria and Josh said in unison. They glanced at each other and quickly looked away, sidestepping their mutual irritation for Gabrielle.

"Don't talk about me like I'm not here."

"Someone needs to speak up for you since you haven't in—" Gabrielle held up her fingers and wriggled her shoeless toes—"thirteen years."

"If you can't be cordial, Gigi, you need to leave. Mama's missing and we're all we have. It makes no sense for us to turn on each other."

"Tell me, little Bro, when have we stuck up for each other?"

"I'm not having this discussion with you in front of Synaria. To answer your question, it's been a long time, but today is a good day to start."

Synaria chomped on her turkey sandwich and enjoyed the Benson antics. For once she silently thanked her parents for being an only child. After calling Gabrielle at Joshua's request, she gaped at the beautiful but arrogant woman Alice spoke of at the library. She waltzed through the front door, barely speaking. She tossed her heavy, expensive coat to Synaria as if she were the maid. A head of healthy, bouncing curls flowed around her face; thank God a fan wasn't blowing because it was apparent Gabrielle fancied herself a superstar. Synaria held back a chuckle at the image of Gabrielle on stage like Beyoncé with a fan blowing her hair. She didn't help put the lunch spread on the table, she didn't set the plates or pour the drinks, and she belittled Alice every chance she got. No wonder Alice was so lonely; she had no refuge with her husband or her family.

"Pass me the lettuce, Sakina."

"It's Synaria."

"Okay, Sy-na-ri-ya," Gabrielle elongated her name. "May I have the lettuce?"

"Sure." Synaria passed the tray of romaine with a tight smile.

"Anyway, since I'm the oldest and have power of attorney over Mama's affairs, I'll decide the next move Alice should make. Judging by the clothes she wears, she can't afford a place of her own right now. Joshua, she can stay here with you until she gets on her feet. She doesn't need to be in an apartment. She's so weak that she'll let Beryl slide back in."

"Gigi, Alice probably wants her own space." Joshua considered his words. "You're welcome to stay here, Sis. I didn't mean to imply you're not wanted in my home."

"I do want my own space. A bachelor needs to be alone. I want to keep my job at the library and find somewhere to stay."

"Alice, you can stay at my home until you get on your feet. I have three bedrooms."

"Thanks, Synaria." Alice pinched off the cinnamon roll near her sandwich. "Gigi, may I stay at the house? I mean until I find something? It's only fair since it is our childhood home."

She sipped her Mimosa again. "Since we're all here together, I wanted to let you two know I'm selling the house."

"What?" Alice and Joshua shouted.

"What do you mean you're selling the house? It's in my name, Gigi. Daddy insisted his son, his only son, keep the house."

Without missing a beat, she hissed, "And since it's paid for, you can deed it to me and we'll split the profits three ways. It could help with my new start."

Synaria folded her arms, enjoying the three-ring circus.

"What new start, Gigi?" Alice asked.

"I'm getting married. Colton and I want to start fresh in our own place."

Synaria jumped in. "Surely you don't mean Colton Bembry? Colton Bembry who recently spearheaded the Bookathon gala with his *wife*, Roselle?"

"They're divorcing soon."

"Didn't look that way to me."

"Why are you involved in this conversation anyway?"

"Because—"

"Forget it! I don't know why I came here in the first place. I should have stayed home." She jumped from her seat.

Joshua stood. "Sit down, Gigi. This bickering is the reason Mama's missing and Alice is here. It has to stop."

She huffed. Sat again. "Do you realize you sounded just like Daddy? Same tone and pitch."

"I was thinking the same thing," said Alice. "Those weekly family meetings in the den were good as long as we weren't in trouble. He knew how to keep us in line. I'd give anything to see both of them again. I miss them so much. The older you get, you look and act just like Daddy."

Josh blushed at their words. "I wish I could be half the man he was."

"With the exception of your relationship antics, you're pretty close." Gigi pushed back her plate and addressed Synaria with, "do you mind giving us some privacy?"

Alice gripped Synaria's arm. "Don't go."

Synaria was in no mood to deal with Gigi's venom. "I was leaving after lunch to get you a few things, remember? I looked at the tag in back of your dress. Size eight, correct?"

"Yes."

"I'm going to pick up a few clothes from the mall and swing by later."

She took her plate and glass in the kitchen, emptied the leftovers in the trash, and headed back to the dining room. "Thanks so much for lunch, Josh."

He rose. "Let me get your coat and walk you out."

Gabrielle and Alice waved to her as she exited the dining room. Josh removed her coat from the hall closet and helped her put it on.

"You mind if I step outside with you?" he whispered.

"Sure."

He closed the door and took the lead. "I meant it when I expressed my appreciation for you bringing my sister here. She's been disconnected from us for so long I thought we'd lost her." Synaria nodded as he spoke, waited for him to finish. "Have you ever tried getting reacquainted with someone?"

"I can't say that I have."

"It's going to be a long road for us."

Synaria felt the same. "I figured as much. She's like a shaking leaf at work, always looking over her shoulder or jumping at the slightest mention of her name. Beryl says nasty things to her when he drops her off, but she always denied there were problems."

Josh clenched his fists. "I want to drive over there right now and handle him."

"Don't. That would make you like him. Maybe this is what Alice needed to start over again. To see him with another woman."

"Maybe you're right." Josh never paid attention to Synaria at the library, but now, he saw her with new eyes. When she removed her coat earlier, he didn't want to gawk, but her voluptuous frame caught his attention. She was well-put together, wearing a gorgeous mauve cashmere sweater and stylish black work pants. Her black booties placed her just beneath his chin. Deep-set, brown eyes enthralled him; they danced with concern as she spoke about Alice. She placed her winter bucket hat over a perfectly highlighted short bob that accentuated her light-brown skin and moon face. Her moist, full lips were moving, but he had to snap out of the trance she'd put him in to hear her. "What was that, Synaria?"

"I said I don't want to buy anything too gaudy for Alice. She's been wearing those croaker sack dresses so long she probably wouldn't be open to anything I purchase."

Joshua pulled his wallet from his back pocket and peeled off $200. "Take this."

"I can't. This is my gift to Alice."

"This is my gift to you for revamping her wardrobe. Mama hated the way she dressed and always talked about it at Grand Oak when I visited. Think of this as your stylist fee."

She moistened her lips and slipped the money in her coat pocket. "I'll be back later. I hope I didn't disturb your family lunch."

"You eased the tension. I'm glad you were here."

Synaria's heartbeat quickened. "See you, Josh."

She walked quickly to her car, erasing the distance between them and ignoring her dry mouth and rising temperature.

14
In Absentia

The siblings sat in Detective Jimmerson's cramped office. They passed the death certificate amongst themselves, weighing the finality of its words.

"Can't we give it some more time?" Joshua asked.

"It's been two months. The state was gracious in allowing so much time to lapse before issuing the death certificate. When a person is missing or presumed dead, a death certificate can be issued within days. We received a few leads about your mother, but nothing concrete came from the tips. Even the sighting of your mom in South Carolina led to a dead end."

"So she's gone. No trace, no body," Alice said, cradling her arms as she rocked. "I'm sure if we wait one more month, she'll turn up."

"I can't take another month. I've lost my appetite and I can't sleep worrying about Mama," said Gigi, placing the death certificate on the detective's desk.

"That's a shock," Joshua muttered under his breath.

"What did you say?"

Alice stopped the impending argument. "Listen, Mama wanted us to attend Emma Jelks's service and we didn't. She wanted us to come to the Christmas pageant and we didn't. The least we can do is have a small memorial service for her. It would be fitting to have it at El Bethel since she attended the church with Ms. Emma."

"Graveside only. I don't want to hear any solos, reflections, or people telling us we have their sympathy," said Gigi.

"You know Mama wouldn't approve of a graveside service. Think about the folks at Grand Oak and the community. Since she left, we've had an outpouring of support from friends and strangers. I'm sure my coworkers and Alice's friends from the library would like to pay their respect."

Gigi agreed, but without emotion. "Fine. Tell me the time and I'll be there."

"We're planning this together, Gigi."

"I can't."

"Do it for Mama, Gigi," said Alice.

She closed her eyes to process Alice's request. After a half-hearted shrug, she mumbled, "Sure."

"I'm sorry this didn't turn out better for your family. Your mother seemed like a wonderful person," said Detective Jimmerson.

"She was, Sir. She truly was a phenomenal mother," said Joshua.

A week later, Gabrielle, Alice, and Joshua sat on El Bethel's front pew with neighbors and friends. Synaria sat next to Alice and offered Kleenex; Karen sat next to Joshua. After a little wrangling, Agatha convinced Gigi to let Zoe sing two solos. Riveted, the crowd remained seated but swayed to her soulful inflections. A soprano, her song rose to the rafters of the stately building.

"Ms. Mattie loved that song," Karen whispered to Josh as Zoe sang, "Goin' Up Yonder."

"She did, Karen."

"She pretended she couldn't sing, but she had a beautiful voice."

Joshua stared at Karen, then redirected his attention to the pastor. He'd never heard his mother sing. From the moment her service was announced in the paper, people shared stories about their mother's generosity that left them speechless. After the benediction, mourners congregated upstairs and in the annex. Earlier, Joshua looked at the tables filled with food, secretly willing them to remain intact. He feared they'd buckle under the weight of so many delicacies.

"We're receiving visitors upstairs since there's no interment," Joshua said to Alice. She'd been distant throughout the service and he worried about his baby sister. He placed his arms around her. "Join us."

"You two stay up here. There are people downstairs, too," she said.

"We'll be down, soon."

She nodded and headed downstairs. Suffocating under the guilt of her mother's death, she wanted to disappear. She waved to familiar faces from Grand Oak and the library, plastering a smile on hers. Tables and chairs were neatly placed throughout the room as people ate and chatted. She knew she should mingle amongst them, but she couldn't. She kept walking, seeking a chair to rest her weary feet.

"That's the baby girl right there," Agatha said, as she walked past. "The other daughter and son are upstairs."

"I'm surprised they had a service seeing as how they didn't come to see about her in the home," said another woman Alice recognized from her mother's hall. "I still shudder at the thought of Mattie's body lying in a wooded area somewhere."

Alice's neck whipped around, insulted by their words. She turned on her heels to address them when someone tugged her arm.

"Would you like something to eat?" asked Roxy Coleman, her parents' neighbor.

"No ma'am."

Mrs. Coleman embraced her. "A group of us from the neighborhood are in back fixing plates and drinks. We set up the head table for you and your siblings. Are they coming down soon?"

"Yes, Ms. Roxy." She took a deep breath, ignored Agatha and her cronies. "I don't have much of an appetite. I'm gonna take a seat until they get here."

She found a seat and engaged the sympathizers as best she could. Amid the "I'm sorry," "Hold on the God's unchanging hand," and "Weeping endures for a night, but joy comes in the morning" clichés, her bowed head rose when a familiar voice said, "Things haven't been the same without you. Please come home."

She jerked in the direction of the voice. "What are you doing here?" she asked through gritted teeth. She shifted in her seat in order to avoid a scene. The din in the room grew louder as people fellowshipped. No one noticed Beryl.

"She was my mother-in-law."

"Who didn't care for you, nor you for her."

"I loved Ms. Mattie. We just didn't see eye to eye on what it means to be head of household."

She yanked his arm and slid into an unoccupied room. She paced a few steps, then faced him. "Beryl."

"What, Baby?"

Beryl's favorite scent, Versace Eau Fraiche, tickled her nostrils. He'd lost weight and wore an impeccable pin-striped suit. He held out her favorite flowers, daffodils.

"You can keep them. I don't want anything from you. Except your signature on the divorce papers."

"Did you have to serve the papers to me at my job?"

"Oh, would it have been better to do it at home with you and Davina present?"

"Alice, I made a mistake. If you come back home, things will be different."

"I'm never coming back there again. I bet it still smells like onions and roses in my house."

His face blanched. "What about your things? You have shoes and clothes at the house."

"I have new things."

Disgust crept on his face. "I see. You look like a Jezebel with that war paint on your face." He closed the space between them. "Where'd you get the dress? Other women dress that way, not my wife."

Alice touched the belt of her navy blue and red apple dress. Mattie loved red and blue, so the siblings each wore outfits in variations of the hues. The dress, ultra conservative and stylish, only outlined her curves. No cleavage was exposed, and the dress fell past her knees.

"There's nothing wrong with my dress."

"It's too short, and a man can see your breasts and hips."

She mock gasped. "Heaven forbid someone took an interest in Beryl Parker's old lady!"

He dropped the flowers, further narrowing their stance. He pushed her against the wall, attempted to kiss her. "You know you miss me. Admit it, Alice." His breath reeked of alcohol. He pushed his tongue slightly forward, licking the side of her face and ear. His hands traveled the length of her dress as he stuck his right leg between hers. He pried them apart and lifted her against the wall.

Incensed, she pushed his chest, scratched his face. "I don't want you!"

"Alice. Alice, where are you?" Synaria's voice moved closer to the door. She pushed the door open as Beryl stepped away, hands dropping to his sides. "What's going on in here? I saw you two walk away when I came downstairs. You disappeared before I could stop you. Is everything okay?"

Alice took a few deep breaths and gave Synaria an unfocused gaze. "I'm fine. Beryl paid his respects and was leaving."

Synaria didn't miss lines of blood trickling down his face. She hoped the scratches were accompanied by a good groin kick. Defeated, he picked the flowers up from the floor.

"This isn't over. I won't stop fighting for our marriage."

"Goodbye, Beryl."

Synaria waited for him to leave. "Alice, what happened?"

Her chest tingled and her stomach clenched. "He tried to…I'm not sure. A part of me misses him, but I know we can't be together again. He's all I've ever known." She fell into Synaria's arms, willing her tears to stop.

"My offer still stands if you want to move out of Joshua's place and live with me. We've got you. All of us."

15
Your Eyes And Ears

Dear Mrs. Benson:

Your homegoing service was magnificent! El Bethel was filled to capacity. People crammed the sanctuary and the overflow. It was awkward without your body, but that was to be expected. We started this thing with the idea of you being gone for the weekend. Just to see if your children would do their best to find you. I thought you were coming back, but I guess I can carry on this game if you're willing to play as well.

Let me tell you something: Agatha's granddaughter is a powerhouse! She may as well have been a charmer and the church members' cobras. She sang "When You Hear of My Homegoing" and "Goin' Up Yonder," as I've never experienced.

Alice, Gabrielle, and Joshua placed a beautiful photo collage of you and Mr. Benson in the entryway of the church. So many of your friends and staff from Grand Oak came that they sat in a section together. Karen sat up front with the family, though. The jury is still out on the eulogist. He did a fine job, but he wasn't needed after people spoke of your kindness, deeds, and commitment to your children. You were a generous woman! I mean you are a generous woman. One woman said you paid her electric bill, another talked about the groceries you purchased, and one man spoke of the gift cards you provided for his family during their quadriplegic son's illness. You were busy indeed.

The will reading, per your instructions, has been set for next Friday at Roastfish & Cornbread. I will keep you updated as to the findings.

On a moral note, there is still time to come back. You can say you wandered away, got lost, was abducted by aliens—okay, I kid, I kid—anything. Your children seem lost without you. I'd hate for you to miss the opportunity of bonding with them again.

You are fascinating, and I'm in your service.

Best,

Your Eyes and Ears

Mattie tucked the letter in her pocket.

"Come back, my foot. They miss me about as much as the Klan wants to attend an NAACP meeting. Maybe they need to see what it's like without their parents."

A light tap at the door broke her thoughts. Refusing to open the door, she vowed to avoid her neighbor as long as she could.

16
I Need Every Dime Of That Money

The lively crowd at Roastfish & Cornbread made the occasion bearable. The ambience—soft music playing, a painter indulging patrons outside the building, chitchat at every table, and children negotiating with parents about menu items—felt like old times. This was Mattie's favorite restaurant, and they weren't surprised when she requested the will be read there.

A waiter escorted them to a private area in back. Gabrielle scanned the room for bandless men, one of whom could be Colton's replacement. He'd sent a flower arrangement to her mother's funeral but had kept his distance since the night of the disappearance. A few men winked and smiled; she gave polite waves.

They sat, gave their drink orders. "I'll be back with the drinks shortly. Attorney Durk will be with you soon," said the waiter.

"Thanks," said Joshua.

"Remember how Mama always took our sweet potato cornbread?" Alice asked.

"She picked on our cornbread and stuck her fork in my fresh catch," said Joshua.

"She sure did. She was a magnet for kids, too. Whenever we were here, a child always came over to show her a drawing or touch her hair," said Joshua.

Alice noticed Gabrielle's reticence first. "Don't you have at least one good memory of being here with Mama, Gigi?"

"We're here to discuss money, not memories."

"I want to get this over with, too. It makes me nervous thinking about getting money from our parents," said Alice.

"Parents are supposed to leave a legacy for their children. You should be happy they set something aside for the three of us. I am glad I won't have to toil away like a slave working for people every day," said Gabrielle. She stared at her phone in anticipation of a response from Colton. The last four texts she'd sent him went unanswered.

"Whoa! Mama and Daddy didn't have money like that, Gigi. Daddy always talked about giving us enough to make us whole and maintain a decent living. I'd be surprised if we had half a million total."

"What? You don't think they gave us a million each?"

Joshua nearly choked on his gum. "In what world do you live?"

"Gigiland. Where no one's feelings matter and it's all about her," said Alice.

"My, haven't we become more vocal since escaping the Parker Plantation?"

"Gigi, stop!" said Joshua.

"She started it by insulting me. Is it so bad men are willing to pay for the pleasure of my company?"

"No, it's bad that you allow them to." Alice smirked.

"You two—"

"Am I disturbing something?" Attorney Durk asked. He stood at the table, eyed his watch, and made a mental note to get back to the beach as soon as possible. The siblings looked at his guest.

"What is she doing here?" Gabrielle asked Attorney Durk but kept her eyes on Karen.

"She's part of the proceedings as well."

The waiter returned with the drinks. Attorney Durk took a seat and the waiter placed a seat at the table for Karen.

"How is everyone?" she asked. Joshua and Alice said hello; Gabrielle continued to stare.

"Drink for you too?"

"I'll have an Arnold Palmer," said Karen.

Attorney Durk had dressed down for the day with a golf shirt and khakis. He'd gone bald since they last saw him. His attempt to hold on to the last of his hair was a topic of conversation amongst them for years. He was their family attorney and they watched in vain as his hairline receded throughout their lives. He'd hit the tanning bed again; his sunburned skin told the tale.

"It's been a while since I've seen you all together. I'm so sorry to hear about your mother's passing."

"She disappeared," said Alice, laying her head on her left arm.

"She is no longer with us and I'm sorry for your loss. Your mother and father were wonderful people," he said.

"She was like a grandmother to me," said Karen.

"I have other business to attend to, so I'll make this short and to the point. This is a very unconventional reading because your mother left personal messages for each of you."

"Really?" asked Gabrielle. "If that's the case, should she be listening in?" She pointed to Karen as her lips curled.

"Actually, a personal message was left for her as well."

Attorney Durk opened his briefcase and removed contents from a large manila envelope. The notes were sealed, and he pulled an unfolded legal document from the folder.

When the waiter set their drinks down, Karen removed the paper from her straw and dunked it in her Palmer. Gabrielle grabbed Karen's hand.

"Where'd you get that ring?"

Karen jerked her hand back. "Ms. Mattie gave it to me."

"Liar! That's the ring Mama asked for before she disappeared. Why would she give *you* her wedding set and not her children?"

Attorney Durk lifted his hands in a cease-fire position. "It will all be explained soon. Be patient, Gigi."

He held everyone's rapt attention as he opened the envelope marked "Karen."

"Karen, thank you for making my days at Grand Oak wonderful. You were more than a CNA, you were a friend. It's like God gave me a chance to go back in time and share sage wisdom with my younger self. Remember everything I told you about family and relationships. Family is the code word for fellowship; make sure you continue to do that with your parents, your brother, and eventually, your husband. The ring I gave you is expensive, the priciest one Daniel ever purchased. When you do get married, use that as your wedding ring and make your husband get you really good bling—isn't that what you called it—on your ten-year anniversary. The traditional gift is tin or aluminum, but Honey, if you can stay with a man ten years in this day and time, by all means, get yourself a fat diamond from him. I also left the rest of the jewelry I wanted you to have in the safe deposit box at Grand Oak. Attorney Durk will see to it that you receive the $50,000 cashier's check I willed to you. Don't stop at being an R.N. Keep going. You can do it, and I hope this helps you along the way."

Gabrielle slammed her fist on the table, spilling a little of her drink. "She coerced Mama into giving her the money! She wouldn't have done that herself."

"Gigi, you know Karen was there for Mama when we weren't," said Alice. "I'm surprised she didn't give her more."

"Speak for yourself! I was there to visit her as often as I could. That dictator you called a husband wouldn't let you see her, so don't judge me."

Joshua piped in. "As long as it was convenient for you, you saw her."

Gabrielle rolled her eyes at Joshua and addressed Attorney Durk.

"Please get to my letter so I can leave. I don't want to be here with these Judases any longer."

"Her instructions were to read Karen's letter first, then yours in birth order, youngest to oldest. Alice and Joshua, do you mind if I change the order?"

"Not at all," said Joshua.

Alice tilted her head in consent.

"Before he starts, I have to go back to Grand Oak for my shift. I'm sorry for the confusion all this has caused. I did nothing to coerce or bribe Ms. Mattie. She loved me and I loved her. Plain and simple."

Karen exited the restaurant as he opened the letter. He cleared his throat and proceeded.

"*Gigi: I apologize for enabling you all of your life. You were our first, and Daniel and I wanted to make sure we did everything right with you. The right schools and the right friends. He treated you like gold, and I stood aside and didn't teach you things a mother should teach her daughter. You grew worse after the incident. All these years you've been living on the flowerbeds of Eve, sleeping with other women's men, taking gifts from them, never thinking of the hurt you caused people. You've gotten by on your looks and charm, but no more. At least not on our dime. You no longer have access to my or Daniel's money, and you have thirty days to vacate the house. Since it is in Joshua's name, he will have to see to it that you leave. No grown-ass, forty-nine-year-old woman needs to be living in her parents' house, even if they're both gone. Get you a job, get you a life, and get a man of your own before somebody's wife sends you to a local funeral home.*"

Heat tinged her face. She muttered, "How did I let this happen?" Her voice grew louder. "All this mumbo-jumbo apologizing and no mention of how much money she's giving me? I need every dime of that money! How am I going to start over?"

She snatched her purse from the chair and left, ignoring her siblings' calls for her to return.

"Attorney Durk, this is a tad heavier than I expected. Do we have to continue?" Josh asked.

"Yes. It's tough but necessary. I wasn't finished reading to her, though." He looked at the time, decided his golf game and trip to the beach were a wash. "Let's take a quick break and come back to the table in ten minutes. Fair enough?"

"Deal." Joshua took Alice's hand and led her outside.

17
If I Could Turn Back The Hands Of Time

A breeze flowed between them as they stood outside. Joshua stuffed his hands in his pants pockets, rattled change, and chawed on his bottom lip, habits he practiced when nervous.

"I can't believe Gigi," he said.

"I know. What incident was Mama talking about?"

"I don't know. Something happened when we she was a teen that no one ever spoke of. Mama and Daddy were so tight-lipped about it that I stopped asking over the years."

She shook away thoughts of her selfish sister. "I can't believe Mama and Daddy. I know we weren't the best children, but I didn't think they'd withhold money from us."

"I don't need their money."

"I do. Beryl isn't taking me or the restraining order I have against him seriously. I don't make much at the library and I need to get on my feet."

"What's wrong with staying at my house?"

"I want my own space. It's something I should have done a long time ago. I feel like this is my punishment for all the money Beryl stole from me."

"What money?"

She sighed. Her family lost track of their religious affiliations over the years, so she didn't bother telling Joshua about the financial scandal. She knew her workaholic brother probably didn't pay attention to anything other than women or his career pursuits.

"Money went missing through the leaders of our last church."

"Went missing? You make the money sound like it was a Lear-jet that flew away."

"May as well have been. Lots of families are suffering. Some people lost their life savings."

"Why haven't you pursued getting it back?"

"I am done with Beryl and the money. If starting over with nothing is the route I need to take, that's what I'll do."

"Let's get back inside. Whenever we see old man Durk in casual attire, it means he's having down time."

In spite of the day's tension, they managed a small laugh.

He stood as they approached the table again. "I was about to come get you two."

"No worries. We apologize for Gigi's behavior. She's been on a roller-coaster ride since Mama's disappearance."

"Understandable. Shall we proceed?"

They nodded. Attorney Durk opened Alice's letter.

"My Baby Girl:

My biggest regret is not spending the last years of my life with you. As much as we tried to snatch you back from Beryl's grip, his influence was too powerful. I watched my bright-eyed, youngest daughter who loved nature, cooking, and fashion waste away in an unloving marriage. Daniel and I tried to be a good example for the three of you, but I guess it's true that children don't always emulate modeled behavior. That's water under the bridge now. When you lived at the house and attended Savannah State, you were a few credits shy of getting your degree. It's time you finish it. You can get financial aid because of your income. Once you get your degree, make sure Durk is aware, and you'll get your inheritance. Daniel and I won't leave you rolling in dough, but you'll have enough to start life anew."

Alice released the breath she'd been holding. She thought her mother would berate her in the letter, but the compassion with which she wrote made her feel guiltier.

"I don't know where to start."

"I'll help you, Alice," said Joshua.

She made a knot on the side of her cotton sundress with her finger. Save church, work, and an occasional drive around the city, she couldn't navigate a college campus again. She'd be the oldest student in the room.

"I don't know if I can do this. Maybe I'm better off without the money." Synaria's voice lingered in her thoughts. *"The first step is always the hardest."*

"Are you ready, Joshua?"

"As I'll ever be."

Attorney Durk opened the last letter. It was the longest of the three. He braced himself for Joshua's reaction.

"Dearest Joshua:

I wonder if you know how proud I am of you and your accomplishments. Not so much that you have a fancy title floating behind your name, but you persevered through dyslexia. You gave us quite a scare when you were growing up. It wasn't until Daniel suggested testing that we figured out why you were always transposing letters and numbers. You preferred being alone to being with a bunch of guys. The few friends you made have stuck with you over the years. Oh, remember how you took the SAT three times until you got the score you wanted? That's Benson tenacity! It is the same tenacity I want you to use to get to know your son. That's right, your son. I've suspected over the years you never married because you didn't get over Deborah Sampson. You all were a cute couple when you dated. She broke your heart when she split, but it wasn't entirely her fault. We may as well have been shit on those high-faluting Sampsons' shoes. They didn't feel you were the right kind of man for their daughter.

In a moment of fear, she confided her pregnancy in me when she called the house to speak with you. She told me how much she loved you, but couldn't keep seeing you. Her parents had her husband picked out. They made her break up with you, promise to get an abortion, and never speak to you again. She went behind their backs and had the baby anyway. He is your spitting image, only lighter: handsome, charming, and smart. His name is Langston Calhoun and he lives in Atlanta. He has her husband's last name. Over the years she sent pictures and kept me updated, but I told her I'd take the secret to my grave as I promised. I never told your father, either. I know this is a shock, and I hope you can forgive me. Of all my children, you are the one who needs money the least. You do need to get to know your son. Find a way to get to know him. He deserves to have you in his life."

Joshua repeated the last sentence aloud. "He deserves to have you in his life." He sat back in his seat. "Deborah Sampson." He rubbed his head and pondered what might have been if he'd known why she rejected him. "If I could turn back the hands of time."

"I have a nephew. Somewhere in this world, a young man is carrying our genes," Alice said to no one in particular.

"Would you like me to help you get in touch with him?" Durk asked.

"I'm not sure. I don't know what to make of this news. I can't go barging into his life, especially if her husband is the only father he's known."

Durk nodded. "The last order of business is the actual assets." He waved the legal document in their faces. "This is to be read once you all complete your assigned tasks." He slipped the letters and paperwork back in his briefcase and stood. "If you two don't need anything else, I'll be leaving now."

"Thanks for meeting with us. I appreciate everything you've done," said Joshua.

They shook hands and waited until Durk left.

"What are we going to do?" she asked. Her eyes darted around the restaurant. She wondered if the patrons heard the conversation.

"I am speechless. We need to tell Gigi, but she's so wrapped up in herself she wouldn't believe us. This plan of Mama's will never work unless we work together."

Alice considered the irony. "Is it me, or do you agree that even in death, Mattie's still calling the shots?"

18
How Do You Sleep At Night?

Gabrielle stuffed the last of the boxes in her Mercedes. Her resentment toward her mother grew as she thought of where she'd go. No way was she waiting thirty days to find another place. Colton would understand her plight and assist her. He'd always been so good to her. He finally agreed to see her at two o'clock in Pooler at the Embassy Suites. Maybe he was finally ready to move along with her and dump Roselle.

Attorney Durk was right; there was no money in the accounts. Mattie either moved it or cleaned it out.

"She always plotted against me," Gabrielle said aloud.

She drove toward Embassy Suites, thoughts of Alice and Joshua crowding her mind. She would be okay if she never saw them again. She visualized Joshua coming to the house with a sheriff, tossing her out and leaving her to fend for herself. Mousy Alice would stand next to him, head bowed and looking stupid, unwilling to defend her.

"Why couldn't I have been an only child?" she said aloud.

None of that mattered. Colton would make a better life for them, set things straight. He made enough money to build a new house far away from the memories of her parents and siblings. Sure, he'd pay alimony to Roselle and support his college-aged children, but that was fair enough. His son and daughter would get used to having a new mother. An attractive stepmother. Why would he want to stay married to that fat pig anyway? She cackled at the memory of Roselle in the thrift shop, barely able to breathe. It was her fault for not satisfying him. Her phone rang, announcing Joshua's call. She answered, frustrated by the sound of his voice filling her car.

"What?"

"Where are you?"

"Taking care of some business. What do you want?"

"Meet us at the house. We need to talk. Besides, there's something I need to share with you."

"I'm sure you can tell me later. I've been banned from the house anyway."

"Gigi, you have thirty days until you leave. Stay there until you work things out. Besides, we need each other."

"You two don't need me, and I certainly don't need you."

"Attorney Durk wasn't finished reading to you."

"I don't want to hear anything else from him or the two of you for that matter. Leave me alone. Pretend you never knew me."

"Gigi—"

She ended the call, annoyed with Joshua. She couldn't wait to hug Colton and give him a deep passionate kiss. They'd spent many nights at the Suites, laughing, planning their future, swapping fantasies of life after his misery called Roselle. She found a space in the self-parking area. Colton always drove and valet-parked them; today, she'd run in and out. She'd practiced her speech about him helping her find an apartment. She needed the day to go shopping for new furniture, curtains, and dishes. She took a few things from the house, but she wanted her new, temporary digs to reflect her tastes. She walked toward the hotel entry, stopping to check her text messages. She beamed when she read Colton's message: *Wait 4 me N the lobby.*

Slipping the phone in her pocket, she walked toward the check-in desk.

Chante, their regular check-in girl, waved to her. "Hi, Mrs. Bembry. I haven't seen you here in a few weeks. How's the Mister?"

"He's wonderful."

Gabrielle felt guilty pretending to be Colton's wife. Chante, an enthusiastic college student, always complimented her clothes, perfume, and looks. Colton nuzzled her neck and held her hand whenever they got a room, so she went along with the lie the day Chante said, "I wished my parents were still married like the two of you."

Without missing a beat, she assured Chante, "A marriage like ours is rare, and I don't take him for granted."

"Where have you been? I haven't seen you all in a while," said Chante, placing her hair behind her ears.

"We've been traveling. I came over to see if he got our room."

Chante pressed a few keys. "Not yet."

"Oh, he's playing games."

"Role playing later tonight?" Chante bent down beneath the counter and rose with a plastic bag in her hand. "You were so right about this stuff. I have an extra one if you need it."

Gabrielle blushed as Chante discreetly removed the K-Y Love Passion gel.

"You *actually* bought it?"

"Yes! My boyfriend loves it. It was the spice we needed to get things back on track."

They giggled as Chante slipped the tube in the bag.

Chante motioned for Gigi to come closer. "Oh, the alum is fire! I did the teaspoon with warm water and put it in the douche like you said. Ms. Gigi, I was revirginized!"

"Don't do it too often. Just enough to rotate your routine, okay." Gabrielle pointed to the lobby furniture. "I'm going to sit over here and wait for Colt. Behave yourself, Ms. Chante."

Gabrielle sat in the lobby area and removed two magazines from her purse. Taking her mother to the doctor and various appointments required patience and entertainment. When Mattie was still with them, she encouraged Gabrielle to keep her favorite books and magazines handy in case the doctors' visits ran over, or if the office didn't have magazines she liked. She skimmed the pages of *Essence* and *InStyle*. Bored with the latest styles and career advice, she closed her eyes momentarily, pondering the scene at Roastfish & Cornbread. She had to find a way to make money. A mild headache formed as she wondered how she'd make things work.

She smiled when she heard Colton clear his throat. She opened her eyes in anticipation of seeing him dressed well and ready for action.

"Ba—"

Gabrielle wanted to be teleported to Mexico. Africa. The moon. Anywhere except the couch on which she sat. Colton and Roselle stood before her, a united front. Roselle held his hand and rubbed his shoulder.

"Gabrielle."

"Colton."

"Let's go over to 145 Mulberry and talk."

"I don't think that's a good idea. I thought we were meeting alone."

He returned Roselle's affection and held her hand tighter. "She is part of the conversation. Let's get a table."

Gabrielle stood, noted Roselle's significant weight loss. Her calm demeanor made matters worse. She'd yet to acknowledge her with a hello or greeting. They entered the hotel's restaurant and were quickly seated by their waitress. Colton and Roselle sat together on the makeshift booth along the wall; Gabrielle faced them in a lone chair.

"I'll give you some time to look over the menu," said the waitress. She placed water and lemon slices at the table before walking away.

Colton and Roselle didn't touch their menus. He spoke.

"Gabrielle, I, we, won't be here long. What I have to say will be brief."

He looked to Roselle for consent before continuing.

"I am publicly apologizing to my wife and to you for what I've done. I've hurt her and we are working hard to get our marriage back on track."

"Her? What about me? You told me you were leaving her and that we'd be together. What about that, Colton?"

Roselle stiffened but remained silent. She rubbed his hand and kept her eyes on Gabrielle.

"Gabrielle, I got caught up. Things had gotten stale between Rose and me and I slipped."

"Damned right, you slipped. And licked. And sucked, and everything else imaginable. Is he like that with you, Roselle?"

"Don't insult my wife!"

"You can, but I can't?"

Roselle cleared her throat. "I'm not intimidated by your kind. I hoped we could be adults about this matter, but I guess two out of three ain't bad. A man can get sex anywhere in the streets, but I challenge you to think of the number of men who really leave their wives for women like you. You are a very beautiful woman, but do you think he'd trust you if you got together?"

He waved the waitress away who'd returned to take orders. Supporting his wife's statement, Colton added, "I am sorry for leading you on. I should have been there for my wife and kids and I wasn't. She knows everything about us, Gabrielle, so there's no need to bring up things we did in the past to hurt her."

"Why bring me here in person? You could have told me this over the phone."

"I'm acknowledging my wrongdoing, and I'm getting closure. I don't want to go back on my word to Rose."

"How charming. It's good to know I meant nothing to you."

"Gabrielle, I'm sorry."

"You don't have to tell me that, Colton."

When she stood to leave, Roselle nudged his shoulder.

"Gabrielle, sit down. I'm not done."

"I'm not a child, Colt. You don't tell me what to do."

"I told you we were one adult short," Roselle said.

Gabrielle plopped down in her seat, scratching the ends of the chair on the floor for emphasis.

"The keys. Give me the keys to the car."

"Colt, that's my only means of transportation."

"Surely a woman of your *caliber* can get a car," Roselle chided.

"Colt, please don't do this. I need that car."

"Gabrielle, the car is being towed as we speak. I'm taking my car back with or without the keys."

"You wouldn't!"

"I did."

A smirk of satisfaction covered Roselle's face. She smiled and took a swig of water.

"Your credit cards were cancelled this morning, and I closed out the account at the bank."

"How am I supposed to live?"

"Working like the rest of us," said Roselle. "Colton has supported you long enough. How do you sleep at night taking money from married men?"

Gabrielle unzipped her purse, chucked the keys at Colton, and ran from the restaurant. She exited the hotel in time to see her car being angled for the tow bed lift.

"Wait!"

Two men orchestrated the tow. Gabrielle spoke to the one outside the truck, read his name tag.

"Marcus, that's my car. May I please get my boxes out?"

"Colton Bembry gave us strict orders to take this beauty away."

"I know. I need to get my things out. Please."

She batted her eyes and gave him her famous mistress-in-distress look. He opened the door and the trunk.

"Five minutes, Gorgeous. Five Minutes."

Seeing her struggle with the car's contents, he helped Gabrielle stack the boxes and bags in the Embassy Suites parking lot. He'd seen a lot of women break under the weight of repossessions and broken-down vehicles, but he knew this situation was different. He wondered how Colton Bembry snagged such a stunning woman. *Must be the money.*

Colton and Roselle made sure the vehicle made it on the tow truck before driving away. Gabrielle flicked her middle finger, whipped out her phone, and dialed Joshua's number.

"Change of plans, Little Bro. You and Alice need to pick me up from the Embassy Suites."

19
Vanilla Ice Cream With Peanuts

They felt eerie in the house without their parents. Gabrielle had stayed in the house so long after they moved out, they hardly recognized it. Now, memories of their childhood rushed back as they stood in the living room.

"Looks like a hurricane hit the house. What did you do, Gigi?" Alice picked up shirts, shoes, and lingerie strewn about.

"I started moving out like Mama asked me."

Joshua assisted Alice with moving the clothes. "You're being pigheaded as usual. What do you not understand about thirty days? That's more than enough time for you to job hunt. Where were you going to live anyway?"

"It's not important." She assisted them with her clothes. "I can't believe Mama would do this."

Alice sucked her teeth. "I guess I'm the only one willing to voice the truth. We let Mama down in her last days. Gigi, you were the worst."

"There you go pointing fingers again."

"We have a short window of time to do what she asked. I'm not playing referee with you two," said Joshua.

"Did you hear that, Alice? He sounded just like Daddy again."

"Daddy. Funny you should say that word," he said.

Joshua sat in Daniel's La-Z-Boy. His countenance caught them off guard; they sat across from him on the sofa.

"Before you got all in your feelings and walked away from the restaurant, you missed something very important, Gigi." He waited for her to look him in the eyes.

"Josh, go ahead and tell her."

"Tell me what?"

"I have a son."

"No you don't."

He sighed. "Deborah was pregnant all those years ago. She was supposed to have an abortion but didn't."

Gabrielle sat upright. "Sweet little Deborah Sampson was having sex? You mean my responsible brother, Joshua, didn't step up to the plate to make things right?"

"I didn't know until today. Mama kept it a secret all these years."

"I'm not following you."

Alice assisted him. "Deborah broke up with him because her snooty parents felt Josh wasn't good enough. She was pregnant by him, they had someone else picked out for her to marry, and the two of them raised our nephew. His name is Langston Calhoun."

"I know damned well they didn't think that about you. You were the best thing that happened to her."

Startled by the rare compliment, Joshua smiled.

"Wait right here."

Gabrielle disappeared upstairs. Alice and Joshua, unaccustomed to the brief moment of camaraderie, braced themselves for the worst. Their oldest sister wasn't friendly or accommodating toward them. Joshua knew something had gone down at the Embassy Suites because he'd never seen his sister look so helpless. Nor had she ever needed him. There she sat in the hotel parking lot in a lawn chair provided by a concierge. Boxes on either side and dejected, their sister had fallen from grace in front of Embassy guests.

"Come in the kitchen, you two!"

"What's she doing?" Alice whispered.

"Probably carving out voodoo dolls of us."

They laughed but honored her request. To their surprise, she sat at the island with a laptop. She navigated the screen in such a way that the three of them had access. She waved them over to the bar stools.

"Remember when we used to do our homework in here?" Alice asked. She took a seat, observing the search engines Gabrielle had pulled up.

"We always waited for Mama to finish cooking dinner. Daddy would pull weeds or tend to the garden outside," said Alice.

"Don't forget—"

"Mrs. Claudine Mitchell's vanilla ice cream," Alice and Joshua said in unison, taking Gabrielle's words.

"Couldn't eat it without peanuts," said Gabrielle. "She brought some to the house this past summer. It's in the deep freezer in the garage."

"Let me get some bowls."

Gabrielle clicked away at the keys as Alice retrieved the ice cream from the garage. What Daniel thought was punishment for the children—being sent to Claudine's place to help make ice cream—turned out to be a summer highlight. Claudine enjoyed the company and the children learned how to make old-fashioned ice cream in an antique churner. They also felt sorry for her; a widow who lived with severe hirsutism, visitors were rare in her home.

"Do we have any peanuts?" she asked. She pulled three bowls from the cabinet, rummaged in the drawer for spoons and a scoop, and set the bowls aside.

"Top cabinet next to the microwave. Mr. Planters himself," said Gabrielle. She typed faster. "I want to see what my nephew looks like."

She waited for the images to appear on the screen. Alice fiddled with Mrs. Mitchell's signature ice cream top as Joshua looked at his son for the first time.

He released a sharp exhale. "He has my eyes."

Gabrielle leaned in. "He looks like you, Daddy, and Grandpa Earl."

Alice lined the bottom of the bowls with peanuts and piled them high with ice cream, the way they all enjoyed it. She took her place back on the bar stool.

"Let me see him." Her nephew stood with the Georgia State University soccer team. "Impressive!"

Gabrielle rattled off information she found from other sites. There were photos of him on Facebook, Twitter, and Instagram. His popularity was evident: he stood in a circle of guys after a winning soccer game holding a trophy; two shapely girls stood on either side of him in a pose at an outdoor concert in Chastain Park; his parents hugged him during graduation.

"Zoom in on that one," said Joshua.

They watched their brother's transfixed eyes. He stared at Deborah and her husband so long, Alice broke the trance.

"You okay, Bro?" Gabrielle asked.

He read the caption beneath the photo aloud. "*I have the best parents in the world! No one compares to Ennis and Deborah Calhoun.*" Sucker punched, his voice grew terse. "Shut it down, Gigi."

"We just got started."

"I've seen enough."

Joshua left his ice cream untouched and returned to the La-Z-Boy. Alice and Gabrielle followed him.

"Now who's all up in *his* feelings?" Gabrielle asked.

"She never gave me a chance to know him. Never hinted she was pregnant. She knew I loved her and she stopped returning my calls, never answered any letters. I would have married her in an instant."

"Doesn't sound like she had a choice in the matter," said Alice.

"All these years. I have a twenty-year-old son and this woman said nothing. I wish she'd put the child support bloodhounds on me. Anything to acknowledge my existence."

"Why don't you reach out to her?"

"Alice, look at how she snuck around with Mama all these years with the secret. I want to have a relationship with him and it's apparent she's not having it."

"You can have it."

"Gigi, the queen of creeping, speaks."

"Alice, I'm not the queen. More like the princess. If he wants to see his son, I say go for it. There is enough information on the Internet to at least lay eyes on your child, Joshua."

"I'm not stalking him."

"I didn't say stalk him. I'm saying get to know him from a distance."

"I want to reach out to Deborah first. That's fair."

"She wasn't fair to you. What exactly did Mama say anyway?"

"She told me he needs to get to know me and I need to be in his life."

"See, you have her blessing from the grave." Gabrielle locked eyes with Alice. "What did Mama tell you to do?"

Alice thumped her fingers on the sofa. "She told me to finish school. I only had a few credits left to get my degree before I got married."

"You don't sound too happy about going back."

"Who wants to be old in a class of youngsters?"

"You're not old. Heck, if Pearl Bailey and Helen Small can do it, so can you."

"Who?"

"Pearl was an actress and Helen was a ninety-year-old woman who got a degree. Mama always spoke of you and them in the same breath. Said, 'If they can go back at their age, Alice has no excuse.'"

"Wow, Mama compared me to senior citizens."

Alice allowed the words to soak in. There was no legitimate excuse for not finishing school. She could have gotten a PhD, been a missionary, and discovered the cure for something after all the stagnancy.

"I know the ice cream's melted. I'll go clean the plates out."

"Alice, I didn't mean to offend you."

"You didn't. I have a lot to think about."

They watched her as she trudged to the kitchen. Gabrielle vowed to watch her tongue. It would take some getting used to, but to get along with her brother and sister, she was willing to try.

"Since you dusted off your pom-poms and can cheer us on, tell us what Mama meant about the incident."

Gabrielle dropped her gaze again. "Joshua, you don't want to know, and I don't have the words to tell you."

Joshua enjoyed the kinder, gentler side of Gabrielle. *Maybe we can make her stay this time.*

20
My Old Basset Hound

The campus had changed so much. Two weeks after Gabrielle shared Mattie's quip about senior citizens pursuing degrees, Alice clutched the Savannah State campus map as Synaria helped navigate the walk between the buildings. They'd been given a tour of the campus, visited the financial aid office, and explored readmission requirements.

"I feel so out of place. Look at these children."

Groups of students soaked up the sun, told jokes, and studied underneath towering Spanish moss oak trees. Alice felt prudish when she looked down at her dress and sandals. Most of the girls wore shorts and T-shirts with the college's logo. Their taut bodies were a reminder of the fact she needed to tone up areas of her body.

"They're adults, Alice. They may be a tad younger, but you all are pursuing the same goal," said Synaria, pulling her from thoughts of inadequacy.

"I don't know about this, Syn."

"Alice, did you forget you can go the e-learning route? You don't have to come on the campus at all. You act like I'm rusty at this game. I'll assist as much as I can."

"By the way, I owe you for the U-Haul van."

"You do. Your payback will be dinner for the next month. I like having company in the house."

"I feel like I'm invading your privacy."

Synaria stopped mid-stride. "If I have to say it a million times, Beryl is no more. You have to get used to starting over. That's what friends are for, to help each other. Stop with this negative talk all the time. It's not a good look. Makes you sound like a victim."

Synaria's candor stung. Alice demanded she take off the kid gloves and deal honestly with her, but sometimes, it was hard. She constantly apologized for little things: spilling juice near the fridge; leaving the lights on in multiple rooms; not folding the laundry in a timely manner—five minutes after she removed it from the dryer was the Beryl Parker rule—and not breaking spaghetti strings in half to make a more robust pot of spaghetti. Try as she might, she couldn't shake the Parker rules. Synaria had been patient, but she feared one day she'd come home from the library and find her things on the front porch.

"Did Jared come by to paint the bathrooms yesterday? I told him you'd be there."

"Syn, I'm so sorry. I heard a knock on the door, but I forgot he was coming."

Synaria held out her hand.

"Synaria, I only have one dollar."

"It's mine. Every time you say I'm sorry, it costs one dollar."

"This is crazy."

"Yes, the way you constantly apologize is crazy."

Alice gave her four quarters, the last of the money in her purse. When they stopped by Joshua's, she'd get the rest of the money she'd hidden in the guest bedroom.

Synaria looked at her phone. "That's why Jared's been calling all morning. He probably thought I changed my mind. By the way, he's safe."

"I didn't think he wasn't. I forgot he was coming by is all. I still jump at the sound of a telephone."

They headed to Synaria's car, chattering away like teens. A few catcalls from the young men on campus made them blush. Alice's adrenaline rushed; it had been a long time since anyone paid attention to her.

"I hope you're not letting this jailbait get under your skin and in your head," Synaria joked.

"I'm thinking about school. These young bucks don't mean anything to me."

"Good, keep it that way."

Synaria drove toward Joshua's. Their morning had gone as planned, and she needed to drop Alice off to pick up the extra car in Joshua's garage. He'd been on her mind and she didn't want to let Alice know the thoughts she'd had of him.

"So he's really letting you drive the 'Stang."

"Shocked me. He knows I don't have a car, so when he offered the key, I said yes. He put me on his cell phone plan, too. This smartphone baffles me, but I'll get the hang of it."

"May I ask you something personal?"

"Shoot."

"How did you live all those years in isolation? No phone. No car. Little contact with relatives."

"You get used to it after a while. Friends and family fall away, then one day you wake up, and your husband becomes everything. By the time Beryl was done with me, I didn't know if I was coming or going." Alice looked out the window, recalled a crazy incident. "One day he told me his grandmother missed me. He took me to her house and left me there two days. I had no clothes and no way to get home. I wonder if he was seeing Davina then. I'm sure he was with someone else."

Synaria caught a glimpse of her sullen face. "Sorry for bringing up bad memories."

"May I have my dollar back? If I can't apologize, neither can you."

"Touché."

Synaria pulled into Joshua's driveway as Alice opened the garage door.

"What time are you coming home?"

"I have a few more things to pack. You and Josh have spoiled me with these clothes and shoes. I still have the housewares I purchased from JCPenney and a few toiletries. I'm taking a nap, then heading in about five. The school tour blew my mind."

"See you later."

She waved Synaria away and closed the door. She placed her shoes on the rack in the garage. It was she who suggested making Joshua's house a no-shoe zone and made him buy a stylish shoe rack from The Home Depot. The pristine carpet in her home remained crud-free for this reason. She tiptoed into the living room, taking care not to awaken her brother. He was asleep on the couch when she left for the campus. He had two more weeks of working from home before returning to the office. He enjoyed the solitude but told her he missed his coworkers. She reached for the remote, then noticed the letter taped to the television. *Gone to meet Deborah. Be back tomorrow night.*

"That sneak! He waited until I left."

She and Gabrielle had begged him to see his son, at least speak with Deborah about getting to know him. The proposition was tricky but worth it; her brother didn't need to walk around with that what-if hanging over his head.

Alice turned on the television, scrolled through the channels. She felt as if she'd died and gone to heaven. It had been years since she'd freely enjoyed television. After a few weeks of reality TV and talk shows, she decided CNN Headline News satisfied her TV jones. She also loved the *Today* show. She set the alarm on the clock near the bookcase for two hours; she'd take her nap, pack her things and go back to Synaria's. She headed to the kitchen to fix a sandwich and froze near the window. She shook off the sight. "Can't be." She wanted to call Synaria, but she had to handle this on her own.

With trembling hands, she prepared a snack, drink, and settled in front of the television. Her attention was drawn to the window again as the familiar car, their car, coasted past her. Her earlier confidence waned. She tossed the pastrami sandwich on the coffee table, marched to the front door and went outside. Beryl put the car in reverse when he saw her on the porch. She neared him but stayed a safe distance as he opened the right window.

"Beryl, why aren't you at work? What are you doing here?"

"It's called a vacation," he slurred.

"You can't be within one hundred yards of me. You know that's the stipulation of the protective order."

"You're still my wife, and I'll see you when I want."

"I'll have Joshua call the police, Beryl."

"He left a few hours ago. So you plan on calling him to call the police on me?"

Her stomach dropped. She suspected he had been watching her. Joshua's neighbors were young professionals who took pride in getting out to work every day. She missed the old days when meddlesome neighbors reported everything to each other and the police. Trapped in her thoughts, she didn't see Beryl get out of the car. He tottered over to her, placed his hands on her shoulders.

"Alice, this isn't you. I said I was sorry. Baby, don't do this to us. I can change."

Alice batted his hands from her shoulders. He smelled as if he'd fallen into a vat of vodka. He'd missed several buttons on his shirt, his pants were unzipped, and his unkempt hair matched his unshaven face.

"Don't you miss me, Baby?"

Images of him with Davina came rushing back. "No!"

"We both vowed for better, worse, richer, poorer, through sickness and health. Did you forget?"

"I'm moving on with my life and you should too, Beryl."

"Is that why you went to Savannah State today? To move on with your life?"

"You followed me?"

He closed the space between them and whispered in her ear, "Looks like my old Basset Hound is working on some new tricks. What will you do with your degree?"

She pushed him away, headed back inside.

Beryl spoke to her back. "Thirteen years of my life gone and you can't excuse one mistake?" The word "excuse" came as an indictment. "All I tried to do was protect you and this is the thanks I get?" His voice cracked on the word "get," and she heard something from him she'd only heard once in all the years she'd known Beryl: crying.

Her feet glued to the front porch. He'd violated the Temporary Protective Order, but something inside her broke at the sound of him crying. The feminist discourse, the vows, the thought of starting over all swirled together like a tornado inside her. She didn't know what to do. Barely able to stand, he staggered toward her back and spilled his tears on her dress.

"Help me, Alice. Please."

"Let me lock the house up, Beryl."

21
Into Thin Air

Joshua stood outside Deborah's pediatric dental practice, unsure of what he'd say to her. Calhoun Pediatrics. The alluring office sign and building were exactly as he expected. Deborah did nothing half-assed, and he knew she'd be successful in whatever career path she chose. He entered the building on Cascade Road determined to complete the task at hand. He was greeted at the front door by a smiling receptionist behind a desk and a little girl who immediately attached herself to his leg.

"Carissa, no! We don't touch strangers," said a woman who pried the youngster from his leg.

"She's okay," he said.

He sat down to catch his breath from the nervousness. Carissa held Ken and Barbie dolls dressed as doctors and ignored her mother. She sat next to him and held out the dolls.

"Barbie had a heart attack and Ken is going to resissitate her," she announced through the space where two teeth once resided.

"I'm sure he'll *resuscitate* her and make her feel better," he corrected.

She placed Ken atop Barbie and made huffing sounds as Ken's stethoscope swung from side to side.

"Carissa, get over here!" her mother yelled.

He scanned his surroundings. The waiting area was reminiscent of an arcade and the sea. Video games nestled against the wall blended in with a blue-and-white mural of floating fish, bubbles, and sea kelp. An elevated treasure chest held colorful toothbrushes, floss, and mouthwash.

"Sir," the receptionist called to him. When he reached the desk, she asked, "What is your name and where is your little one today?"

"I'm Gary Ames. I have a ten o'clock appointment. I mentioned I wanted to speak with the doctor before bringing Gary, Jr. in."

"That's right. I remember now. I still need you to fill out insurance information for me. If you'll take this clipboard, we'll get you processed as soon as possible."

He filled out the forms with bogus information. All he needed was ten, fifteen minutes alone with Deborah to plead his case. If he could see Langston once, he'd walk away and never bother them again. He had so many questions, he didn't know where to start.

"Mr. Ames, come on back," said a hygienist.

He followed her to room three.

"Dr. Calhoun will be with you in a few."

Before-and-after patient photos lined the wall. The children smiled as Deborah hugged them or held out a piece of fruit. She was as beautiful as he remembered, and he still melted at the sight of her smile.

"Hi, Mr. Ames, it's so nice to meet—" She stopped midsentence when she saw him and locked the door. "Joshua?"

"Deborah."

She waited a few beats. "I saw the Mattie's alert a few months ago. I wasn't sure if authorities found her. I see they didn't."

"We had a memorial service a few weeks ago."

She dropped his chart on a station next to the faucet. "Ms. Mattie was something else. She kept the secret all those years."

"I'm surprised you kept the secret all those years. How could you do that to me, Deborah?" He didn't realize he'd raised his voice until Deborah jumped.

"Not here, Josh. I've got patients and a ton of paperwork. How about dinner tonight? I promise I can explain everything. I've been prepared for this day for twenty years."

"What about your husband?"

"He's out of town on business until next weekend."

"May I meet my son?"

"Not yet. Now's not the right time."

"When will it be?"

"We can talk about it."

He sighed. His practiced speech turned dusty on his tongue. He had choice words for her, but he couldn't speak them. They were nasty and mean-spirited. Years separated them from their last encounter, but he sensed she felt as badly about things as he did.

"I'll rip up this fake info, Gary Ames." She scribbled an address on back of a prescription note. "See you at eight tonight."

Joshua rang the doorbell of the upscale condo. He'd bought her pink roses after remembering those were her favorites. She opened the door wearing an apron.

"Hi, Joshua. Come in. Lasagna's almost done."

He followed her and the aroma of good food. His mouth watered at the smell of his mother's lasagna. She had given Deborah the recipe when they were students; he was amazed she kept it all these years.

"Hang your jacket up in the closet," she said, pointing to a door beyond the foyer. She took the roses and headed toward the kitchen. "Make yourself at home."

Her condo was as stylish as the dental office. A huge portrait of Deborah, Ennis, and Langston sat on the fireplace. Order ruled the atmosphere. He watched her trim rose stems and put them in a crystal vase. She spoke over the running water, "I won't bite. Join me in the kitchen."

"Where's a bathroom so I can wash my hands?"

"Your mother's gone but not forgotten. I was always washing my hands when I came to your house."

They both laughed. He washed up and fell in step with her, setting the table and inspecting her wine collection. After placing the gooey lasagna and breadsticks out, he said grace.

"You look nervous. What's wrong?"

"I'm not too thrilled about being in another man's house when he's not home."

"Our house is in Snellville. This is the condo we bought when we married. I stay here when I have a full schedule or don't feel like driving to the house. Our house is an empty nest anyway."

"I see."

"You don't have to worry about him barging in on us." She sipped wine. "Should I be worried about Mrs. Benson? Ms. Mattie refused to discuss your personal life with me, so I never knew if someone else snagged your heart."

"Not even close."

"Come on. No one?"

"I've been engaged a few times. Never made it to the altar."

"You were a good guy. I always wanted you to find the right woman."

"You were the right woman for me." He sipped more wine. "Let's cut to the chase. Does Langston have a clue Ennis isn't his father?"

"No. Ennis is all he's ever known. That was one of the agreements we made before we married."

"So you two shut me out without any say? Deborah, you disappeared into thin air."

"I didn't shut you out. My parents did. My mother never forgave me for going behind her back and having Lang. She took forever to bond with him, and she felt I ruined my life in the process. My goals took a little longer to accomplish since I had a baby."

"How are your parents anyway?"

"Mom died of cancer four years ago. Dad's still a golfing widower."

"Does this mean I have no chance to get to know my son?"

Deborah rubbed his arm and took his hand in hers. "I didn't lie to you when I said Ennis was out of town. The issue is *where* he is."

Joshua didn't want to break her momentum, so he remained silent.

"He's in rehab. In Arizona. Cocaine was his mistress for years, then he finally went ahead with her. Daddy spent so much money covering for him and getting him out of trouble. I think Mom died from a broken heart. She was sure I had the perfect husband and it didn't turn out the way she planned."

"Langston knows this?"

"Yes. He's already disappointed in Ennis. I can't spring you on him right now. He feels betrayed by everything that's happened since he graduated."

He pushed away from the table and stood. "My timing's way off. I'm not sure what I thought I would accomplish by coming here."

"I knew this day would come. I've been waiting for you to come back. I was afraid your mom would slip up and mention Lang. It's hard to forget your first, Joshua." She stood as well.

He faced her, caressed her cheek. "I never stopped thinking of you, Deborah. I know we can't have a relationship, but I'm willing to pay back child support. Would you at least allow me that privilege?"

"No. That wouldn't be fair under the circumstances. I do well for myself and Lang. Until Ennis's fall from grace, he was a visible political figure here. The rumor my parents concocted is that he's working in the private sector."

"This is too much for me. I'm leaving, Deborah. Sorry I interrupted your life."

She followed him to the closet. "You don't have to go. Where are you staying tonight?"

"Downtown. I'd planned to be here a few days, but I'm going back to Savannah."

"Give me a few days. Please. I'll come up with something."

She followed him to the front door, not wanting him to leave. Seeing him stirred up feelings she'd forgotten. He was still handsome and chivalrous.

"Call me when you get to your room, Joshua."

"Will do. It was good seeing you again."

22
Did You Bring Your Own Bags?

Gabrielle coasted Daniel's Bonneville into a parking space at Target and waited. Job hunting had changed since the good old application days, and she was not pleased. She held a job at a call center twenty-five years ago; the call center manager rescued her by dating her and telling her she was too beautiful to put up with the stress of answering phones. She'd held a string of jobs but stopped working altogether after being dissatisfied with the job market. The nepotism. The pecking order. The gossiping, backstabbing coworkers and the short lunch breaks. She couldn't understand how a person could work thirty-plus years, have a retirement party, then waltz off into the sunset after giving a company they didn't create all those years and energy. Now, she realized a pension and insurance weren't so bad. She'd run into the store, get her items, and go back to looking for a job.

An odd feeling had overtaken her again; she missed Alice and Joshua. She stopped short of trying to bribe Joshua into letting her stay in the family house. It was time to blaze her own trail. She'd missed so many opportunities in life, and she didn't want to spend another day imposing on others. Not her siblings, not anyone else's spouse. Joshua had fronted her money to buy a few items and offered his place until she got on her feet. She'd spent the last week tossing items men she dated had given her. Each trinket was a reminder that she could be bought, and she didn't want to take the remnants to her new life.

She entered the store, grabbed a cart, and greeted the employees who welcomed her. She'd made a list of items that would look good in her new apartment after spending time on Target's website. She was overwhelmed by the home, furniture, and patio selections, so she decided to start with bedding. She spotted the section, turned down the aisle, and froze at the argument taking place.

A middle-aged woman with a radio attached to her hip struggled to keep her hands to her side. She clenched and unclenched her fists as she raised her voice at a younger woman with green hair shaved on one side and a hanging ponytail on the other.

"Katisha, let me make this clear. Your job is customer service. If we don't have the item in stock, you can look in the system to see if it's available at another store!"

"Ms. Bertha, the customer ain't always right. The item she had on that iPad didn't come from our store. It came from Anthropologie. I saw it on a décor blog."

Katisha smacked her lips, flicked her blue fingernails, and turned her face away from Bertha, revealing an intricate lotus flower tattoo on the right side of her face.

"Katisha, the item isn't the issue. You don't speak to customers in that tone."

"She raised her voice at me!"

"Katisha, in my office. Now!"

They trekked off toward the back of the store, Bertha leading the way. Their red shirts and khaki pants finally disappeared in a sea of athletic gear.

"Hey, I'm sorry about that," said a gentle voice. "May I help you find something?"

Gabrielle, lulled back to the aisle, looked at the woman. "I need a nice bedding set and some curtains."

"Do you have a picture of what you need?"

"Yes."

She gave the woman a printout of the set. "Threshold. I love the pinched duvet. This looks good in any room."

She followed the woman to the next aisle over, not wanting to be rude but yielding to curiosity. "How tall are you?"

"Six three."

"Whoa! Basketball player in high school?"

"College too. Wanted to play in the WNBA, but I busted my knee."

"I'm sorry."

"Don't sweat it. It actually led to my true calling. My fiancé and I are opening a bicycle store. This is my part-time gig until we can get things off the ground."

Gabrielle read her name tag. "Good luck with your new venture, Nanette."

"Thanks. What's your name, Miss?"

"Gabrielle. My family calls me Gigi, though."

"I apologize for the argument you walked up on. Most of us in our department are embarrassed about Katisha's actions. I'm amazed she still has a job. She's very good at what she does, but her attitude sucks. She could be a store manager if she gets her 'tude in check. "

"She's young. She'll probably grow out of it."

"I'd lose my job in a heartbeat if I spoke to my superiors that way. I bet she paid someone to take that assessment for her."

"Assessment?"

"Yea. Most of jobs online these days require you to answer all these questions. Employers want to see where your head is. What would you do if? How do you feel about? We were joking in the break room the other day about Katisha's reactions to the questions. I'm sure she sucked her teeth like she always does and said something like, 'Hell naw.' 'How the hell would I know?' 'What you think I am?'" Nanette laughed at the memory of the coworkers' conversation.

"Oh. I've been out of work so long I probably wouldn't pass, either, so I'm not going to slam Katisha." The thought of working frightened her, but she asked anyway. "Are you all hiring right now?"

"Yes. You can go over to one of the computers and do an application."

"Not after you scared me about the process."

"Consistency. Be consistent."

Gabrielle waited for clarification.

"The moment you start the questionnaire, be consistent with your responses. Be confident as well. No one wants a wishy-washy employee."

"Let me finish my shopping."

Nanette placed the duvet in her cart. "We have some gorgeous curtains that would look great with it. Do you like solids or are you into patterned designs?"

"Patterns."

Nanette led her to the curtains. They chatted like old friends and she appreciated her eye for design and knowledge of the store's stock. Eyeing the full cart, she whipped out her calculator to tally everything. She didn't want to be embarrassed at the checkout.

"Thanks, Nanette. Is there a way I can let someone know about *your* good customer service skills?"

They laughed again.

"Gigi, when you get your receipt, complete the survey. You'll have a chance to mention my name."

She pushed her cart toward aisle three. A surge of self-assurance coursed through her veins. Nanette helped her find clearance merchandise that suited her tastes, so she'd have extra money for lunch. Nanette had also solved the mystery of why she'd been doing a lousy job on her online assessments: inconsistency.

Familiar laughter a few aisles over caught her attention. She followed the belly laugh to check out aisle six and saw Colton kneading Roselle's shoulders. He laughed again and leaned in to her. He'd whispered sweet nothings in her ear the same way when they were alone. Roselle closed her eyes and swatted his hand away, joining in the laughter. Her eyes watered at the sight of them.

"Miss, did you bring your own bags?" the cashier asked.

She shook her head. "I'll take plastic."

"Did you find everything you needed?"

"Yes."

The cashier rang up everything, smiled, and marked a circle at the bottom of her receipt. "Have a great day and don't forget to complete the survey."

She stuffed the survey in her purse and parked her cart near the closest computer. She knew she couldn't spend the rest of her life taking handouts from men. She set up a profile, filled out the questionnaire, and exited the store. Gabrielle reflected on the years she'd wasted, the promises that left her dangling in anticipation of having a good relationship like her parents. She placed her bags in the trunk, sat in the car, and released a long overdue cry.

23
Dumber Than A Box Of Rocks

Synaria dialed Joshua's phone for the third time. "Has she returned any of your calls, Joshua?"

"Not yet."

"I can't shake the feeling that something bad has happened to Alice. She didn't come to work today, and she hasn't been back to my house in two days. I told the branch manager she was sick."

"Don't worry. We'll find her. I'll be there in fifteen minutes to pick you up."

Joshua dialed Alice's number again. Voicemail. He dialed Beryl's home number with no luck. He felt uncomfortable leaving her alone at his place to go to Atlanta. She'd made so much progress moving in with Synaria, reenrolling in school, and getting her life in order. Always closer to Alice than Gabrielle, he knew no harm had come to her. He could feel it. When he saw his Mustang in the garage, he knew she'd left the house with someone she knew. He'd promised himself he'd keep his composure. He couldn't afford to be arrested and lose his job, but he didn't know how he'd handle things if she'd gone back home.

He reflected on his meeting with Deborah. Twenty years had passed and she still had a place in his heart. He'd left Atlanta without seeing Langston, but he'd come up with a plan to see his son soon. Alice was the order of business right now. He rang Synaria's phone.

"I'm close to your house."

"Ring the doorbell. I'm changing my clothes now."

He made it to Synaria's subdivision in record time. When he parked, Mattie and Daniel came to mind. If he could see them, talk to them again, he'd want to know how to handle everything going on. As the only son, he'd downplayed his father's mandate that he be the man of the house should something happen to him. He now felt the weight of his father's words, felt responsible for his sisters. Gabrielle had been job hunting and preparing to move out. He couldn't get a handle on Alice's emotions. Maybe Beryl's abuse had taken such a hold on her that she couldn't break free.

Synaria didn't wait for him to ring the doorbell. She opened the door and ushered him in. She gave him a quick hug and asked him to be seated.

She slid her feet into decorative sandals that matched her red jeans and blue chiffon blouse. "I didn't mean to blow up your phone. I won't be able to sleep tonight until I know she's safe."

He eyed Synaria. "I'm just as concerned as you are. I have a feeling she's back home."

"I know. I called you because I didn't want to go there alone."

"It will be fine. She probably won't answer the door."

"Promise you'll keep your cool when we get there?"

"I can't promise, but I'll do my best."

Synaria went to the kitchen. "I need a drink. I made my famous lemonade. I have to swig something."

She prepared two glasses and set them on the coffee table.

"One for me, one for you."

He extended a tight smile and sat back on the sofa. Their family had been down this road with Alice for years. Rescue attempts proved futile. Now another person would witness his sister's vulnerability.

"Have you ever fought Beryl?"

"Once." He paused before sharing the event. "Daddy was still alive. Alice called me in the middle of the night crying and screaming. She'd locked herself in the bathroom with a cordless phone and said he wouldn't let her go to bed unless she recited some scriptures."

Synaria shook her head.

"I called Daddy and we drove over there. I practically beat the door down until Beryl answered. He snatched the door open, said he was the boss of his wife and his house, and told us to get the hell off his property." Joshua's jaw tightened. "I punched him and knocked him down. Daddy didn't stop me, and I would have continued if Alice hadn't interfered. Can you believe she jumped on *my* back and yelled at me to get off him?"

She listened intently.

"I didn't speak to her for two months. He didn't press charges, but I was so mad at her for being foolish. At the time I felt like she was dumber than a box of rocks."

Synaria held his hand. "We had a representative come into the library from one of the shelters a few months ago. It's not uncommon for a victim to go back to an abuser numerous times."

"I learned firsthand."

"Once she makes up her mind, she'll leave for good."

"It's been years."

"It can always happen. Don't stop believing."

He sipped the lemonade and relaxed. Synaria's presence eased the tension. He reached in his jacket pocket and removed a small box.

"I brought you something from Atlanta."

Her face flushed. "What on earth? You didn't have to bring me anything."

"A little bird told me you loved *The Wizard of Oz* and collected figurines. This is my way of saying thanks for all your help with Alice."

She removed the wrapping paper from the box. She squealed after seeing the musical figurine. "You have ESP. This was next on my list to purchase."

The musical figurine featured ToTo and the words *"There's no place like home"* painted on the side. She turned the crank and "We're Off to See the Wizard" played.

"This one goes on the shelf, Joshua. I love it."

He watched her walk to a shelf filled with ornaments. If his personal life wasn't so tangled, he'd ask her out. She was pleasant and down-to-earth, the kind of woman he desired. His mind quickly turned to his past failed relationships, causing him to grab his keys.

"Let's get going. I want to get this over with."

They drove to Alice's in silence. They pulled into the driveway and approached the door with caution. Joshua rang the doorbell five times. They turned to leave and were stopped by the sound of the door cracking.

"Yes."

Joshua eyed his sister. The light that glowed in her eyes at the prospect of being free again had dimmed. She looked at him and Synaria as if they were strangers.

"Who's at the door, Baby?" Beryl asked.

"Josh and Synaria. I'll be back in the house in a few minutes."

"Let them in."

All three raised their eyebrows. She stepped aside and invited them in. Her hands trembled as she offered them seats. They waited for Beryl to join them, but he stayed upstairs. Joshua cut to the chase.

"Why didn't you answer our calls?"

"I feel like I'm a burden to you all. My place is here with my husband. I took vows and I need to honor them. Every marriage goes through a rough patch."

"This isn't a patch, Alice; this is a garden full of weeds," Joshua said through clenched teeth. "You can't be serious!"

"He said he was sorry and he would change. We are going to counseling."

"Alice, he cheated on you. I was here the day you ran out in tears," Synaria added.

"The Bible says the Lord will restore the years the locust hath eaten."

"What about the money he stole? I'm willing to help you get back on your feet, Alice. Come back home with me tonight. You can come back to the library and we can get you going with your online classes." Synaria wrung her hands, desperate for Alice to say she was joking.

"Synaria, thank you. Keep the things you have there. I am Beryl's helpmeet. He wouldn't have slept with Davina if I had been more attentive to his needs."

Joshua had heard enough. He jumped to his feet and approached Alice. "Locust this. As far as I'm concerned, you're dead to me! Our parents didn't intend for us to be out here alone, but if you don't want to be bothered with us, I'll leave you alone for good!"

"Joshua!"

"Don't Joshua me, Synaria. Let's go!"

He headed for the door with Synaria close behind. He gazed at his sister once more, unfazed by the tears streaming down her face.

"Joshua," Alice said. She followed him, touched his shoulder. He slammed the door without acknowledging her.

She hadn't noticed Beryl had come downstairs. He stood in front of her and caressed her face. "He made up his mind, Alice. Let him go," said Beryl.

24
Your Eyes And Ears

Dear Mrs. Benson:

The plan has jumped off the track a little. Things didn't go very well when your children met with Attorney Durk. Gabrielle stormed out of Roastfish & Cornbread, leaving Joshua and Alice in a tizzy. Oh, Gabrielle wasn't too pleased with you giving Karen jewelry and money, either. They didn't like the conditions of the will, but it appeared they were willing to move forward with the plans. Appeared is the operative word here. Joshua hasn't made much progress with meeting Langston, Gabrielle is still job hunting, and sadly, Alice has returned to her husband. There is still time for you to come back home. We can work our way around the whole Mattie's Call thing. These children need you. When something changes, I'll update you.

Your Eyes and Ears

Mattie slapped her thigh in disgust. This isn't how she planned things. Sure, she wanted her children to realize how hard she and Daniel had worked to give them a solid foundation. Isn't that every parent's goal? She figured she'd go away for a weekend, have them go crazy with worry, then show up again since Gabrielle harped on her occasional forgetfulness. Then the Mattie's Call happened, and she didn't know how to stop the scam. Things happened so quickly she didn't have time to retract things. "Oh well, they'll have to depend on each other until I figure this out."

She rocked in the chair Daniel had made for her and reminisced on the times they had shared in this house. He believed children shouldn't know everything about their parents. The Helen, Georgia, property was the biggest secret they'd kept from them and was now her refuge and hiding place. She gathered uneaten apple slices and a jar of peanut butter and headed toward the kitchen.

Daniel promised they'd have a place of their own to keep their romance alive. They'd both been eye-and-ear witnesses to unloving marriages, and they didn't want the same for themselves. He listened to his father's tales about the wealthy family for whom he chauffeured and decided if he ever got married, he'd build a place for Mattie so she could take a break from the real world every now and then.

A knock at the door halted her steps. Many of the people they'd befriended over the years had sold their properties, rented them out, or died. They were cordial to the other residents, but never too chummy and only addressed people on a first-name basis. No histories or trench stories were ever shared. She'd avoided her new neighbor for the past few months she'd been at the house. She was a persistent presence and Mattie decided to face her like a woman and send her on her way.

"Just a minute," she said.

Mattie tied a paisley silk scarf around her hair and put on a pair of sunglasses. Whenever she ventured into town or watered her plants, she took care to be incognito. Even though she was in the middle of nowhere, anyone could spot her.

She strolled to the front door. "Yes."

"I wanted to introduce myself," said the voice on the other side of the door.

She tightened the scarf and opened the door with a tiny crack.

The woman held a garden trifecta in a painted basket: tomatoes, okra, and several ears of corn. Her thinning, white hair jutted out like a weather vane and framed her overdone face. A red headband held medium-sized curls in place. Mattie zoned in on her right eye: its cloudiness gave the appearance of milk that had spilled on her cornea. She wore blue jeans, work boots, and a T-shirt that read "Will Hoe for Vegetables." Animated kale, spinach, and red peppers with legs danced around on the shirt as the caption "Dig Me" hovered above them. She reminded Mattie of a senior Barbie the way her breasts emphasized the veggies. The woman extended a wrinkled hand to Mattie and spoke through Botoxed, ruby-red lips.

"Ursula Kinsey. I promised I wouldn't let this week go by without meeting you."

"Nice to meet you, Ursula. My name is Ma—Maude Benefield." Mattie was amazed at how quickly she concocted the lie.

"Mind if I come in? I have a few vegetables from my garden for you."

Ursula extended the basket and Mattie accepted.

"I'll leave my boots on the porch if that's okay with you. My shoes are a little dirty and I don't want to track mud in your house."

"That will be fine. Come on in and have a seat when you're done."

Ursula may as well have been a cat the way she glided in and sat. She bounced her socked feet up and down on the carpet and removed a pack of cinnamon red hots from her jeans pocket. "Would you like a few, Maude? It's my new habit since I chucked the cancer sticks." She tossed a handful of candies in her mouth and made suckling sounds.

Mattie looked up at the box of candies. "No thank you."

She gave a slight thump to the okra and tomatoes as she rinsed them in the sink. "These are beautiful. I'll shuck the corn later tonight. I haven't had succotash in a while."

"Is that what you'll do with those?" she said, moving the candy around in her mouth.

"Sure will. Succotash is a Southern staple."

"My son, Riley, could never hold it down, so I stopped making it."

"May I offer you something to drink or eat?"

"Water will be fine. Although at my age, it'll run through me like slop through a hog."

Mattie laughed. "Ice?"

"Please."

She left the garden bounty to air-dry and joined Ursula with the water.

Ursula sipped. "I've been seeing you go back and forth and thought you might need some company. I'm shocked you're getting around so well since the grocery truck delivers food to you. The truck is usually reserved for those of us who have problems moving." She swiped a coaster from the stack on the table and set the glass down.

Oh God. Gladys Kravitz. "I like the convenience of the truck. I haven't fired up my Caddy in a while."

"I'm available to take you into town if necessary."

"I couldn't inconvenience you."

"No trouble at all. We're the only three on this path and need to look out for each other."

"Three?"

Ursula flicked out her red tongue and nodded. "Yes. Old man Phillips lives in a house way back off the beaten path. He comes every year in the heart of the summer. Been sick lately, though." She sipped again.

"Oh. I didn't know there was someone else back here."

"May I ask a favor?"

Mattie hesitated. "Go ahead."

"Would you take off your sunglasses? Eyes are the window to our souls and I want to see what you look like."

Mattie leaned back. "My cataracts won't allow it. That's another reason I don't get out all that much. The sun is vicious on my eyes."

"I don't blame you. I'm familiar with eye issues. I was teased as a child and given the name Cyclops. I didn't pay them any mind, though. No childhood regrets and no sitting onstage with Dr. Phil."

Full of new lies brimming on her tongue, she threw out another so Ursula would leave. "I was about to take my nap before you came, so if you'll excuse me."

Ursula stayed planted in her seat. "A few more questions and I'll go. Would you indulge me?"

Mattie sighed. If a few more questions would do the trick, she was onboard. She nodded.

"What brings you to Helen? I bought my cabin two years ago and I'm seeing you for the first time this year."

"It's family property. We don't get up here that much."

"Where are you from originally?"

"Athens."

"I was born and raised here in Helen. Lived in Manhattan until my husband passed two years ago. I decided to come on back home. Things have changed with the town being so touristy now."

Mattie wouldn't give an inch. She stretched her arms and patted the rocker's hand-sewn cushion.

"I'll be going now, Maude. Maybe we can swap recipes sometimes. I'm getting back into cooking after eating out all those years. I'm a yell away, okay."

Mattie lifted her body on the side of the rocker and walked Ursula to the door.

"When would you like your basket back?"

"It's yours. Keep it, Maude."

Mattie bid Ursula farewell and closed the door. Not only would she have to be on the lookout for the police, she now had to contend with Ursula. The longer the handle on the spoon with which she fed her, the better.

25
Father Or Daddy?

Still reeling from his anger toward Alice, Joshua hit the road. Two days had passed since his sister chose her husband over her family. Again. He'd planned to drown his sorrow at a local bar, but he found himself on I-75, playing the scenes over in his mind. First, his mother's death, then Alice's return to Beryl. Surprisingly, Gabrielle seemed to be the warm spot in his life. She did honor Mattie's request to find a job. She was so proud of her job at Target she didn't know what to do. He offered to help her get a job at Gulfstream, but she said she wanted to ease back into the working world, get used to a routine. He didn't expect that much from Gabrielle; it was Alice who disappointed him. He prayed she'd stand up to Beryl, but she cowered underneath the weight of being on her own. People would lop off an arm, a leg, and both ears to have her support system, yet she had spurned them again.

He pumped the music in his SUV, accelerated his speed. If Alice wouldn't be aggressive with a second chance, he would. He felt like a stalker scrolling through images of his son. He was a fool to leave Deborah a few nights ago without a concrete meeting plan. Langston was his son, not Ennis's. He rehearsed his speech to Deborah over and over. He'd request Langston meet his sisters, visit Mattie's grave, and get to know his side of the family. He had a few cousins his age, most of them in the Macon, Georgia, area, but he could arrange a meeting for them all. It would be an impromptu family reunion.

Two-and-a-half hours later, he parked in Deborah's driveway. Ennis wouldn't be back for two weeks, and he'd probably drive to Snellville. For all he knew, she was there too. *What am I doing?* He restarted his engine, then froze when he saw movement drift by the curtain in the downstairs window. He looked at his watch. Twenty minutes was all he needed to convince her to meet Langston. The hill leading to her condo seemed steeper this time. He rang the doorbell, anticipating Deborah's beautiful smile.

"Hi. May I help you?" Langston asked, holding a game remote control. His eyes roamed the space behind Joshua as if he expected others to join him.

Staring at the younger version of himself, he paused.

"Lang, who's at the door?" a deep voice called out.

A string of excited voices blended in with a video game. Joshua peered into the living room and saw a group of young males tapping away at game controls, shouting, and egging on the leading players. He refocused his attention on Langston.

"I'm here to see Deborah. Is she here?"

"Dad, there's a man here to see Mom."

Joshua inhaled. He couldn't turn back now, so he waited for his nemesis to reach the door.

"Hi, may I—"

Joshua glimpsed Ennis. His casual attire—sweats and an oversized hoodie—didn't suit him. Even dressed down, Ennis Calhoun's distinguished presence wasn't lost on him. He understood why Deborah's family had arranged their marriage. Still, he wasn't leaving without speaking his mind.

Ennis stared him up and down, unable to control the fury slowly overtaking him. He turned to Langston. "Let me chat with this old friend of ours. Get on back in there before Dallas beats you down in Fifa."

"As if," joked Langston. He gave Ennis their secret handshake and went back inside.

Ennis slammed the door and walked to the gazebo area. He paced, then turned to Joshua. "I know damned well you didn't darken my door with your presence. How did you get this address?" His voice was a growl.

Unaffected by Ennis's bravado, Joshua raised his voice. "I came to see my son."

"You want to say that again?"

"The last time I was here I didn't get a chance to make arrangements with Deborah about seeing Langston."

Ennis rubbed the back of his neck and blew out a string of short breaths to gain control. "The last time? What do you mean the last time? You've been here with my wife? Are you sleeping with Deborah?"

Joshua sneered and rankled Ennis's nerves with, "You should ask her what's going on."

Ennis pushed Joshua's chest, knocking him back a few spaces. He advanced toward Joshua, his chin high, grinding his teeth. "Any man can father a child, but it takes a real man to be a daddy. What are you, father or daddy?" His raised his fist to punch Joshua's face but instead, grasped his chest. He fell forward on Joshua, his shortness of breath apparent.

Frightened, Joshua held onto Ennis as he hyperventilated. He managed to get him down on the ground. "Stay with me, Ennis. I'm getting Langston."

Joshua ran to the door and beat it until Langston and his friends came out. Langston darted toward Ennis, Joshua close behind. He knelt to his dad and asked Joshua, "What happened?"

"Call nine-one-one, Langston!"

"No! He's having a panic attack. Help me get him inside. I know what to do."

Joshua, Langston, and Dallas hoisted Ennis's body and carried him inside. The living room became a makeshift emergency room as Langston took off Ennis's hoodie.

"Belly breath, dad. Come on, Enny C, you can get through this." The calmness with which he spoke to Ennis gave Joshua pause. No blood between them but so much love.

As he rubbed his father's arm, he said to Dallas, "Go to the upstairs bathroom and bring the bottle of Ativan."

Dallas rushed upstairs, retrieved the bottle, and went to the kitchen for a glass of water.

"Concentrate on your breathing, Dad. In and out."

Dallas uncapped the bottle, pouring two pills in Langston's hand. Langston sat Ennis up and dropped the meds in his mouth like a bird feeding her babies in a nest. Water fell down Ennis's side as he gulped hard. Langston wiped his face with his T-shirt sleeve. They all watched as his labored breathing settled.

"Tell me what you need now, Dad."

Ennis shook his head and laid cold, steely eyes on Joshua. "Leave."

"Dad, who is he?"

Ennis squeezed out the word once more. "Leave. Leave my family alone."

All eyes pierced Joshua as he walked out of the condo.

At the Swainsboro exit, her calls came back to back. He answered, ready to endure her wrath.

"What were you thinking, Joshua?" she yelled.

"About my son."

"I told you I would introduce you when the time was right! You knew what was going on with Ennis."

"Don't you understand my position?"

She sighed. "I apologized for keeping you in the dark. Lang told me how he handled Ennis's panic attack. He loves that man so much. Are you that insensitive that you were willing to blurt out the truth? What would you do if someone told you Mr. Daniel wasn't your father? How would you take the news?" After the lengthy pause, she said, "Exactly."

"Deborah, I came to see you and talk about arrangements. I meant—"

"Your intentions were loud and clear. I don't have a perfect marriage, and the last thing I need to do is make things worse."

"At least let me—"

"Come near us again and I'll get a restraining order against you."

26
Smile And Be Personable

"Gigi, one more note like that and you'll be the CEO," said Nanette.

Katisha sucked her teeth and chomped her turkey sandwich as they sat in the break room. She twirled her ponytail around her finger with her free hand and addressed Nanette. "Once the newness of the job wears off, she'll be sick of these customers just like we are."

Nanette shook her head at Katisha's salty attitude. "You're being hateful, Katisha."

"I'm not. You know how people are all gung-ho at first, then fall off the longer they work."

"I've been out of work for a long time. Getting back into the swing of things has been good."

Nanette needled Katisha more. "Don't you think it's commendable that at least three customers have taken the time to send personal notes to the store about Gigi's performance?"

"Probably corporate plants."

"Still, that means she's doing a good job regardless of who's watching."

"Whatever."

Katisha popped the top off a Tupperware container of fresh, sliced peaches. Her hair and nail colors this week, burgundy and fuchsia, were tamer than the last rainbow. She grabbed a few peaches with her super-long nails and wolfed them down.

"Slow down. We have time before we get back to the floor."

"Nanette, I'm eating so I can smoke before I go back." She wiped peach juice from her mouth with a napkin.

"You smoke?" asked Gabrielle. She didn't mean the question to sound so judgmental. Her face flushed as Katisha's lips turned upward.

"*Yes.*" Katisha's terse response drew air from the room.

Gabrielle backpedaled. "I didn't mean to offend you. I'd never seen you smoke, that's all."

"I guess you'll be the smoking police, too. What with all your *exemplary* qualities."

"Katisha, what's up with you today?" Nanette asked.

Katisha abandoned her uneaten food, yanked her purse from the coat hanger, and poured Kool-Aid from a Styrofoam cup into the sink. She stalked out of the room.

Nanette and Gabrielle stared at each other. Seconds passed and they giggled at her antics.

"She's doing the most today."

"Gigi, don't pay her any attention. Some days she can be semi-nice, other days it's like she spent the night in a hornet's nest. She's so rude."

"Why does she still have a job?"

"She knows the system well enough not to go off the deep end. She works the points system to her advantage, and she does adequate work. Nothing above and beyond, though."

"That must be tiring."

"Wait 'til she gets back from smoking. She has no idea you all are working in Women's Clothing together."

"Oh no. Who told you that?"

"I overheard Bertha telling Herb she could learn a lot from you."

"I'm not in the mood for this today. I can't influence anyone."

"I sure hope you'll rub off on her." Nanette scanned the room and leaned in to Gabrielle. "Gigi, she's on probation and doesn't know it. Three more incidents and she's out." Nanette made a cutting gesture across her throat. "You're attractive and a customer magnet. I don't know what it is about you, but customers are drawn to you. They tell you their business, take your advice."

"I follow the general customer service rule. Smile and be personable."

"When was the last time you saw Katisha smile?"

"Never."

"That's what I'm talking about. All the coaching and talk-withs haven't worked. I tried to be a fly on the wall and listen to Herb when he was talking about her, but he lowered his voice when I was near. There's a reason they've kept her this long. I don't know what it is."

Gabrielle shook off the notion of mentoring Katisha. "All I can do is try to help her. She may be too far gone."

"Hey, nothing beats a failure but a try."

"Say that again."

"Nothing beats a failure but a try." Nanette wadded up her Burger King bag and tossed it in the trash, basketball court swish style.

"My mother used to say that phrase all the time."

"Used to?"

"Yes. She died a few months ago."

"I'm sorry to hear that, Gigi. Had she been sick?"

Gabrielle rarely discussed Mattie's disappearance. For all the conflict they'd experienced, she missed her mother, ached for her. She'd give anything to hear Mattie laugh, to spit out a piece of advice or wisdom, to put her in check.

"Do you remember the woman who disappeared from the nursing home?"

"The Mattie's Call woman?"

Gabrielle nodded. "That was my mother."

Nanette took Gabrielle's hands and caressed them. "I'm so sorry." Fury crossed her face. "I would have sued that nursing home for every dime."

"We're looking into it. We're trying to get adjusted to not having her anymore."

"A lot of people here were talking about the incident. I read her obituary and my heart went out to you all. I didn't realize you were one of her three children."

"If I could see her one more time. I have so many things to say to her. If your mother is still alive, Nanette, cherish her. You only get one."

"I know and I do. You don't have to tell me twice. There is no woman in the world like Mrs. Alva Jean Coles."

They didn't hear Katisha walk in. "I hate to break up the love party, but we need to get back to the floor."

The three of them headed to the floor and were stopped by Herb. "Katisha and Gabrielle, may I speak with you?"

Nanette gave Gabrielle a sheepish grin and headed toward electronics.

"Katisha, you will be working with Gabrielle in Women's for the duration of your shift."

"No hell I won't!"

"Katisha!" Herb and Gabrielle said in unison.

"I've warned you about your tone, Katisha," Herb chided.

She rocked back on her heels. "Before lunch, I was almost done restocking the frozen meats. Why would you make me go to another department now?"

"Last time I checked, I was your boss. Also, you need to be cross-trained."

Katisha put her hands on her hips. "That's way too much people involvement!"

"You need to have a variety of skills if you want to keep the job, Katisha. Gabrielle is good with customers and could teach you valuable pointers."

"Oh, so somebody here less than two months can teach me how to do my job?"

"Coaching, write-up, or suspension if you don't go. Take your pick," said Herb.

Katisha's lips tightened in an angry line. She rolled her eyes and made a beeline to Women's. Herb and Gabrielle followed her.

Gabrielle ran her finger through her hair. "Are you sure you want to do this, Herb?"

"It needs to be done. She has a short time to turn things around or else…"

Stifling her desire to pry, Gabrielle interrupted him with, "I'll work with her. Nothing beats a failure but a try."

27
One Hand Washes The Other

Alice wiped off her desk and took the last of the books and snacks she'd left at the library.

"This resignation feels funny."

"I could have brought the box to your house."

"I've been missing you, Syn. I haven't warmed up to anybody in years and I wish we could go back to the way things were before I went back home."

Synaria gave Alice a warm bear hug. "We're all waiting for you to come back. The library is different now that you're gone." She'd tread the waters lightly. After the night Alice chose to stay with her husband, she immersed herself in reading about domestic violence. She wanted to show support by not blaming Alice or pushing her away. She wouldn't mention Joshua, either.

Alice's face blanched. "You all haven't missed me." She avoided eye contact with Synaria.

She lifted her chin. "We have. Especially Sabir Martin."

"The genealogy buff?"

"Of course. You always assisted him with research. I was a little offended when he wouldn't accept my help."

Alice chuckled. "I forgot about him."

"Don't forget Mrs. Martha Wide. You're the only one who could calm those rowdy grandchildren of hers during story time. She credits you for lighting the spark that now makes her oldest granddaughter read voraciously."

"That wasn't me; that was Harry Potter for Melissa. Remember how the baby girl, Marta, fell in love with Virginia Hamilton's stories?"

"Don't be so modest. You are a valuable member of the team."

Alice sighed and placed a watch in her box. They'd planned to get a replacement battery at the mall on their lunch break a few weeks ago. They never went. She picked up her belongings and headed toward the exit with Synaria. A sense of longing gnawed at her as she watched patrons check out books, job hunt on computers, and sit in study groups. The library was her escape; being home didn't compare.

Synaria snapped her out of the daze. "How did you get here? Is Beryl waiting outside for you?"

She hesitated. "I drove."

"Really?" Synaria didn't realize how loud she'd gotten until someone shushed her. She lowered her voice. "Since when have you started driving places in the family car?"

"I've been doing lots of new things."

Synaria swallowed hard in an attempt to mask her skepticism. "If this is what you want, I'll support you." She stopped short of offering her house again.

"Synaria, I know you and my family aren't happy about my decision, but Beryl is changing." *So am I.*

"It's your life, Alice." *I don't want to see you dead on the six-o'clock news.*

"I have to get to my two-o'clock appointment, so I'll be going now."

Synaria walked her to the car. "Keep in touch. We need to do lunch like old times."

"I will. As a matter of fact, I'll have you over for lunch at my house, so we don't have to spend any money."

"Promise?"

"Promise. I'll even make my legendary strawberry cake for you."

She waited until Synaria went back inside the library and drove off. Excitement and electricity filled her body. She knew they all thought she was pitiful, but she wasn't poor Alice anymore. Beryl was so caught up in their "kiss and make-up" honeymoon phase, he hadn't noticed the subtle changes in her. His indiscretion with muskrat Davina had given her unbelievable leverage. He handed over the car keys, took her out to dinner, and hinted at getting a Cialis prescription. She blushed at his advances outwardly, but inside her master plan was underway. By day, she logged on to Savannah State's website with the laptop Beryl had purchased for her and took classes toward her degree. No longer did he dole out thirty dollars a pop to her; he gave her his credit card and asked her to get her hair and nails done. He complimented her and told her it took almost losing her to realize how much he loved her, how important their marriage was to him.

Humph. I'll show you love. Her phone rang as she took the Statesboro exit. When his name flashed, she answered.

"Are you near?" he asked.

"Yes. Harvey's parking lot, correct?"

"Yes." A few seconds passed. "See you soon."

She ended their call and drove a few more miles. She saw his Infiniti parked in the grocery store lot. She pulled up in the space next to him, waved, and waited. When he cast nervous eyes on her, she instructed him to let his window down. "Do you want me to get in your car?"

"Sure." He eyed people walking in and out of Harvey's.

She slid into his car and wondered if Gigi met men in parking lots. He was more handsome than she remembered when they attended church.

"I'll make this quick. I have to get back home soon and I want to know if you're going to help me."

"Did you bring the evidence?"

"Not so fast. Are you in?"

"Depends on what you have in mind."

"Robert, I didn't want to do this. I was in the dark about everything, too."

"I never thought Davina would cheat. I thought I provided a good life for her."

"Is that why you introduced us to that charlatan who took our money?"

Robert caressed the steering wheel. He'd become a pariah in Savannah since the Ponzi scheme. He arrived at church a few Sundays ago to changed locks and scowling faces. His members no longer trusted his leadership and put him out. He had been fleeced along with his congregation and lost a significant amount of money. Davina promised she'd be by his side, but she'd grown as distant as his flock. When Alice called him to say she'd caught Davina with Beryl, he didn't want to believe her. Curiosity got the better of him when she said she had evidence.

"I apologize for what happened. I thought I was doing everyone a favor. I'd seen other churches flourish and I wanted my members to prosper as well."

She wanted him to offer a better explanation. When he didn't, she asked, "What's going on with the investigation?"

"He's still in hiding."

"I had a bad feeling about him the moment he set foot in the pulpit."

Robert shook away the thought and returned to the reason for the meeting. "About Davina. What evidence do you have?"

Alice opened her purse and removed a small plastic bag. She gave

Robert the wedding band and engraved bracelet. His face fell as he touched the ring.

"She took them off upstairs. I scared them, so she forgot to pick them up. You hadn't noticed it was missing?"

"I've bought her lots of sets over the years. This one was the most special, though. I gave her this set after my father died. She'd been so helpful toward him as he transitioned. I wanted to show her how much she meant to me. The rings, trips, and gifts over the years were my way of letting her know her barren state didn't bother me."

"She can't have children?"

"Nope. She also has a glandular issue, hence the odor."

"You've been with her through all that?"

"I'm no saint, but yes. I love Davina. She put up with my philandering in the beginning of our marriage. When I said for better or worse, I meant it."

Alice sat back in her seat. She wasn't into breaking up marriages. A part of her wanted Robert to hurt as badly as she'd been. Looking at his face now, she felt regret. She shouldn't have called him. She touched his arm.

"I feel like I've ruined your life and your marriage, Robert."

"I've had a hand in both. Don't apologize. I felt Davina was tipping out. I just wasn't sure who it was. You've endured a lot, too."

"How so?"

"I'm not blind. I saw the bruises when you attended church. Sometimes I wondered if you were wearing shades to be fashionable or if something else happened behind closed doors."

Alice looked away from Robert. "I had no idea anyone noticed."

He cupped her face and turned her head to face him. "Maybe it's time we both moved on. I'll broach the subject when I get home since I'm moving out."

"Don't say anything yet."

"Why'd you call me here?"

"We can help each other, Robert. We're both in a position to have a fresh start."

He gazed into her eyes. "What's going on in that beautiful head of yours?"

"Robert Crenshaw, one hand washes the other. Let's lather up!"

28
Speaking Of Traumatized

"There has to be another approach, Joshua. I don't agree with the way you showed up unannounced, but he is your son."

"Gigi, that's why I've extended my leave. I can't concentrate on work right now."

"Deborah won't answer your calls at all?"

"Text messages or emails, either."

"Damn, lil' Bro. It's like she's fallen off the face of the earth again."

She removed the last of the dishes from the dishwasher and put them in the cabinet. The morning's breakfast was her best attempt yet at Mattie's blueberry waffles. She'd gotten a stash of her mother's handwritten recipes from the house and had tried a few new ones the past two weeks. She and Joshua had grown closer since Alice's decision to remain with Beryl was cemented. When she got ready to sign the lease on a new apartment, he insisted she stay at his house until she saved more money. She needed the extra time since she hadn't saved much, but she didn't want to impose on him. Their conversations were awkward initially, but soon they swapped tales about Target, relationships, and their parents. His melancholy state about his son wasn't lost on her; she cleaned, cooked meals, and tried to ease the desire he expressed to see his son. Langston filled their discussions each day.

"Do you know how hard it was to look at him without fessing up?" Joshua wiped down the cabinets and the stove.

"I'm glad you didn't. He would've been traumatized."

"I want my son to know I exist."

"He will when the time is right. We'll come up with a way to smooth things over with Deborah and Ennis."

"I'm not begging them for anything."

"Josh, I didn't say beg. There's a solution. Give me some more time to think."

"Speaking of traumatized, have you talked to that *dumb* sister of ours?"

"Josh!"

"She is!"

"Don't talk about her. She's a victim."

"Victims don't have a way out, Gigi. Our sister had a job, a place to stay with her friend, and a new support system to help her transition. And what did she do?"

"Victims go back to their abusers up to seven times."

"She can stay with him."

"We have to get Alice out of the situation."

"I'm done with her. Change the subject!"

Gabrielle pursed her lips. "You brought her up. No need to be so testy!"

Joshua sat at the kitchen table and massaged his temples. "Everything is so different now that Mama and Daddy are gone. I never imagined I'd be this distant from Alice. I never imagined I would have gotten closer to you. It's like the universe is playing tricks on us."

Gabrielle joined him at the table. "Every night I dream of them. Sometimes I hear Mama's voice. Other times I see Daddy calling us inside from jumping on the trampoline or running through the sprinklers."

"He called *us* in. You were too cute to play with us."

"Touché."

They laughed. Gabrielle's cell phone interrupted their trip down memory lane. Herb's name flashed on the screen.

"Hi, Herb."

Joshua watched as they chatted briefly. She nodded, shrugged, sighed, then eyed her watch. She stood, still speaking with an exasperated look on her face.

"I can be there by two, Herb."

She ended the call.

"What's wrong?"

"Katisha called in again."

"The Ghetto Bird?"

"I never called her that, Joshua."

"You didn't have to. Burgundy hair. Glodean White fingernails." Joshua snapped his neck and repeated the phrase she'd shared. "No hell I won't!"

Gabrielle tried to hold in her laughter, but she couldn't. She quickly regained her composure. "I'm going in to do this job in the hopes she pulls things together. Nanette says her job's on the chopping block, and I pray this isn't the last straw."

Joshua turned serious. "Gigi, you can't justify the kind of action you told me about. If she's missing days, being reprimanded, and doing subpar work, she doesn't deserve a job."

"I know. Everything you've said is true except for the subpar work. She's been improving since being in the women's department with me."

"I like the sound of you being a good influence on someone."

"You don't have to tease me, Josh."

"I'm being sincere, Gigi."

The compliment made her pause. "Thanks."

She grabbed her keys and headed out. She had enough time to sit in the parking lot and meditate before going in.

29
Whatchu Doing Back Here?

Gabrielle plugged in the auxiliary cord, turned on her MP3 player, and listened to her favorite Earth, Wind & Fire jams. Purchasing a new car was number two on her to-do list. She was grateful for the use of her father's old car and even happier Joshua equipped it with a somewhat modern sound system for Mattie when she was alive, but she wanted a newer system like the one in the Mercedes. "All those years of being the other woman and I didn't have flea sense to save anything."

She shook away the memories of trips, jewelry, and luxurious hotel rooms. Her Target stint hadn't been long and she wasn't making a lot of money, but the joy she derived in going to work, meeting the customers, and contributing to the store's success gave her a measure of satisfaction. Her dad's words came back to her: "honest work for honest pay is the only way to go." She smiled at the memory of her father and stopped at the next light. A burst of bright pink hair grabbed her attention as she drove on. Alongside the street, the young woman paced back and forth on her cell phone, her red shirt and khaki pants familiar to Gabrielle. The tan mini-van's hood was open as smoke formed mini clouds. She drove her car in front of the van, parked, and got out to help. Katisha's pace slowed when she recognized Gabrielle. Tears streamed down her face as she pleaded with the other person on the line.

"Mama, I don't know what happened to it—"

Gabrielle heard yelling on the other end, then silence. Katisha redialed the number with no luck. She crammed the phone in her pocket.

"Katisha, let me help you."

"I don't need your help!"

"It's obvious you do. I can take you back home if you need to go."

Katisha's tears came faster. "I can't pay you. I got to get—" She couldn't finish her sentence as she looked toward the van.

"Listen, I can call a wrecker to tow the van and I can take you home. You don't need to be in the middle of the—"

Loud moaning interrupted Gabrielle. Her gaze shifted to the child in the middle seat. Only now had she noticed the accessible lift that had been lowered on the open door. She followed Katisha to the side door and watched her get in. She unraveled paper towels from a roll and wiped the boy's face. He rocked back and forth in his seat as Katisha wiped the last of the drool trailing his chin. She seemed oblivious to Gabrielle's presence as she readjusted his seat belt and his small glasses. Gabrielle took in the fresh scent of his outfit and the care Katisha had taken with his appearance.

"Look in the bag and give me his ointment," Katisha said to Gabrielle, pointing to a diaper bag in the front seat.

She gave her the ointment and watched as Katisha rubbed the side of his ear. Her nurturing way as she soothed him wasn't lost on Gabrielle; this side of Katisha made her feel guilty for speaking negatively about her.

"Did you mean it when you said you'd give us a ride?" she asked, wiping her face.

"Of course, Katisha. I didn't realize…I mean, I didn't know you had a child with—"

"Cerebral palsy. Kirby is four. No one knows except Herb, and the only reason he knows is because his granddaughter attends the same learning center."

Gabrielle remained silent, happy the mystery had been solved. She, as well as the other employees, wondered why Katisha was able to keep a job with her attitude. Martha in produce had quipped, "I don't care what she's got going on; they wouldn't let me work if I came in acting like that!"

"Do what you need to do to get him in my car. I'll call the wrecker and get the two of you home."

"Thank you, Gabrielle."

She scrolled her contacts and found the family wrecker. She knew Mr. Manfield wouldn't charge her anything, but she'd give him $80 for coming out. The retiree didn't come around as much since her parents' died, but she loved him and his wife, Ameila, like surrogate parents. Katisha lifted Kirby from the seat, gathered his wheelchair, and walked him to the car. Gabrielle nodded and paced as she explained what was going on to Mr. Manfield.

"Hold on, Mr. Manfield. Katisha, you'll need to give me your keys. Mr. Manfield is towing the van to his son-in-law's shop."

"I can't afford to get it fixed. Mama's already mad it broke down. She just had it fixed last week."

"We'll take care of it for you. Give me your keys and sit in the car with Kirby."

Thirty minutes later, Gabrielle found herself engaged in conversation with a calmer Katisha.

"Where to?"

"Yamacraw Village."

Gabrielle maintained her composure. She'd just read an article in the paper citing a lower crime rate in the notorious housing project. It'd had its fair share of news coverage surrounding thefts, murders, rapes, and mayhem. Daniel had mentored a young man from there years ago. Whenever he took him home, he never allowed them to ride with him. He made them say a prayer for his safety and asked them to watch over Mattie until he returned.

"How long have you been living at Yamacraw?"

"Since my parents divorced about twelve years ago. After Daddy left, Mama wasn't the same anymore. Living with Mama helps me take care of Kirby and her." She looked at him in the booster seat and smiled. "You think less of me 'cause I live in the 'Craw?"

"Of course not. I'm not here to judge you."

She looked out the window, then redirected her gaze at Gabrielle. "I bet you and your husband have a big, fancy house out in the suburbs, don't you?"

"I've never been married."

"You got kids?"

"No."

Surprise covered Katisha's face. "Ms. Gabrielle, I thought for sure you were married with kids. I figured that Target check was your Victoria's Secret money. A lot of ladies your age get out the house 'cause they're bored and have nothing else to do."

"My age?"

"I didn't mean anything by it. You look real good. I just figured you were around my mom's age, that's all."

"I wasn't offended. How old are you?"

"Twenty-five."

"I am old enough to be your mother. I'm forty-nine."

"I was guessing forty. Mama's forty-four. She married my daddy right out of high school. Had me at nineteen."

"Wow!"

She eyed Kirby again. "Kirby's Daddy was my high school sweetheart, too. We were both going to college just before I got pregnant. After I had the baby and he was diagnosed with CP, Kirby, Sr. denied being the father and left. He said his sperm didn't produce retards."

Gabrielle cringed at the word 'retards.' "Did you take out child support?"

"Look, if a man doesn't want to claim his own flesh and blood, I'm not going to force him."

"But the money could help you and your son, Katisha."

"You sound like Mama." Katisha pointed right. "I'm on the next street over."

Gabrielle turned on the street and parked alongside the curb.

"Our unit is on the end with the ramp."

Katisha placed Kirby in his wheelchair; Gabrielle carried the diaper bag. Katisha tapped on the door and yelled, "Open up, Mama!"

"Whatchu doing back here? I told you to call Lois and have her pick you up!" The door flung open and a small woman stopped her tirade at the sight of Gabrielle. She pulled the housecoat she was wearing tighter and smashed out her cigarette in the ashtray she held. She fussed with the blue sponge rollers in her hair. "Who is she?" She held her stance at the front door.

"This is my coworker, Ms. Gabrielle. She gave me a ride home."

"You gonna miss pay. They wouldn't let you come in late?" The scent of alcohol lingered after she spoke.

"Mama, it's hot. Let us in."

She stepped aside as they entered the small apartment. Gabrielle was knocked off her feet by the surroundings. With the exception of a Jack Daniel's bottle and a highball glass on the coffee table, the space was immaculate. The smell of beans, neck bones, and cornbread wafted throughout the apartment. Katisha parked Kirby's wheelchair near the sofa.

"Have a seat, Ms. Gabrielle, while I talk to Mama in private."

Gabrielle took stock of Kirby, who'd fallen asleep. She wanted to pick him up, but she was never good with children. They either spat up on her clothes or pulled her earrings. There was something different about Kirby, though, and he warmed her heart. Ten minutes later, both reemerged from the bedroom: Katisha in a headscarf, T-shirt and jeans; her mother clothed in a Chevron maxi dress.

She'd taken the rollers from her hair, revealing a halo of fluffy curls. Katisha disappeared with Kirby as her mother took a seat across from Gabrielle.

"I'm Rowena. What do I owe you for bringing Tish home and towing the van?" She reached inside her bra and produced a thick wad of bills from her bosom. "My boyfriend, Larry, just had it fixed last week and the doggone thing is down again," she slurred. She scratched her pimply face and licked her thumb.

"You don't owe me anything." Gabrielle wanted Rowena to stop peeling off bills. Her chipped, yellowing nails smelled of cigarette smoke as she counted twenties.

"Nothing in life is free. This is part of my rent money, but I can't let you drive all the way over here and not give you something." She pressed the wet bills in Gabrielle's hands.

"Katisha has been doing a good job at work and I want to make sure she keeps working."

Rowena poured Jack Daniel's in the high ball and took a swig. After a brief moment of silence, she said, "You might not believe this, but I used to be a retail manager. Had two stores back in the day." She held up two fingers as her red eyes danced at the memory. "I keep telling Tish jobs are hard to come by and she better do a good job at Target. She's had an attitude ever since Kirby Sr. left. I keep telling her another man will accept her and the baby, but she won't listen."

Gabrielle gave her the money back. "Consider this a gift." She eyed her watch and stood. "I have to get to work myself since I'm covering for Katisha. The man who towed her van should have it done in a few days. If Katisha needs a ride, I can pick her up since we've been working together."

"Beloved, you are an angel. Do you want me to scoop up some of these beans and cornbread for you in a Tupperware bowl? I haven't had time to cook the okra yet, but you're welcome to it."

Beloved? Okay, Iyanla. "No. I have some lunch in the car. It was nice meeting you, Rowena."

Rowena staggered a bit and regained her footing. "I wish you didn't have to go. I miss having company with ladies. All my friends are like the wind, Girl. They've blown away. You seem real nice."

"So do you."

"Tish! Your friend is leaving. Come say goodbye to her."

Katisha practically ran from the bedroom. Her eyes were downcast as she walked Gabrielle to the car.

"This is between the two of us, right?"

"Katisha, I would never tell anyone at work what happened today."

"I know I get on people's nerves, but I'm dealing with a lot. Between trying to keep Mama sober and taking care of Kirby, I don't have a life. Target is all I got."

"Do you want me to talk to Herb? He is an understanding man, especially since he knows about Kirby."

"Tell him I need a little time to get my transportation together."

"I can pick you up."

Katisha grew silent. "I can't pay you back right now."

"You don't have to pay me back. Consider it a favor."

"Nothing in life is free."

"My generosity is." As Gabrielle turned to leave, a thought popped in her mind. She faced Katisha again. "On second thought, you can do something for me, Katisha."

"What?"

"Let's work on that hair and those nails."

30
I Have Lots Of Regrets

"Ursula, you are a godsend. I don't know how I would have gotten through my day's running around without you."

"Maude, I am at your service. All we have is ourselves back here. I'm starting to think old man Phillips doesn't want to be bothered with us."

Mattie gazed at the winding trail to his property. "I don't think anyone lives there. He's a ghost."

"That old coot is back there. He's cheap and stubborn. From what I was told by the previous owners, he's never been one to socialize." Ursula unpacked the trunk of her car and placed Mattie's bags on the porch. "Do you want these inside?"

"I've got 'em. They aren't too heavy. Besides, I need the exercise."

Ursula eyed her watch. "You joining me for the evening news?"

"You know how I feel about that idiot box."

"Come on, Maude. I'm not for all the reality shows, but it's good to know what's going on in the world."

"Don't try to hold me hostage all night, Ursula."

"Well, at least a good ransom would be paid for you. You're the other person I know who shops with cash only in this day and time."

Who needs the paper trail? "Don't take offense to this Ursula, but there was a time we couldn't get a credit card, mortgages, or anything having to do with a bank. We weren't considered trustworthy. Banks felt we wouldn't pay anything back." Mattie put her groceries away and fanned herself with an old-fashioned church fan. Grateful she'd stockpiled the safe in the cabin with cash, she felt blessed that she'd remained self-sufficient. The last thing she needed was to be tracked down after withdrawing money or making a debit purchase. She was sure Gigi sent her death certificate to credit card companies so she wouldn't have to pay the small but outstanding balances.

Ursula bristled at the word "we." We? Moments like this crystallized their differences. Ursula avoided the topic of race like the plague. Maude was one of many black people she'd befriended and she genuinely enjoyed their camaraderie. If her mother knew how close she'd gotten to Maude, she'd tsk and tell her she'd gone too far. Because of her mother's racist rants growing up, she and her husband taught their son not to see race, but growing tensions with police brutality and murders made her extra-sensitive during their conversations; she watched her tongue during their excursions. Race really didn't matter to her as a child, and certainly not as an adult.

"How long are we going to be at your place?"

"We can watch the news, *Wheel of Fortune*, and *Jeopardy*. I'll walk you back down. I'll even whip up some of my popcorn."

"You and your popcorn."

"Admit it, air popped is better."

The ladies trudged to Ursula's cabin and sat in front of her huge flat-screen. Mattie loved the coziness of her place and the way she made her feel at home. Guilt inched its way in her heart again. Her end of their friendship was make-believe. She wanted to admit her crime to Ursula, but she wouldn't understand. Lately, she tossed and turned at night, wondering how her children were. She stopped opening mail from the private investigator; it was painful reading how they'd gone on with their lives. Their situations were rocky, but they were moving on. Twice she dialed Joshua's number but hung up on the second ring. No words could adequately describe the hole she felt without her family.

Ursula set a bowl of popcorn on the coffee table and squirted cherry syrup in their glasses of Sprite.

"Which news program tonight, Maude?"

"CNN. We always alternate between *Nightly News* and CNN." Mattie's bladder swelled. "Headed to the little girl's room. I'll be right back."

Mattie settled in with a magazine from Ursula's rack. She flipped a few pages of *More* and froze when she heard, "She should be stoned leaving her family like that!" She clutched the towel rack, unsure of how she'd explain herself. The story had died down months ago. Who brought it back up again? She cleaned up and rejoined Ursula.

"Maude, can you believe this?"

Mattie breathed a sigh of relief when she sat down. The breaking news story read "Missing Pennsylvania Woman Reappears 11 Years Later in Florida Keys." She looked at the woman's photos placed side by side: the one on the left showed a vibrant, attractive housewife. The photo on the right showed a woman who appeared destitute and homeless. Her distant, cold eyes begged for something. Ursula's full-blast air conditioning made her tuck her legs under a small blanket.

"You wait eleven years to turn yourself in?" Ursula asked the TV. She grabbed the remote and turned up the volume.

Immediately, Mattie homed in on the broadcast details. She noted the irony of the missing woman's last name: Heist. She'd stolen eleven years of her family's life. Finances and a pending divorce made her walk away from her family, her life, and her problems.

"Brenda Heist should be ashamed!" Ursula's irritation grew. She flipped the channel to TV Land.

"Turn it back!"

Ursula did as Mattie asked but shook her head as more details emerged. Ursula munched popcorn and spoke to Brenda as if she could hear her. "Denied housing assistance, my ass! You don't leave small children."

"Maybe she was scared."

"You make it work. Do you know how many single mothers use the system for its intended purpose until they get on their feet? She didn't try hard enough."

"I think she—"

"Shhh. The husband is talking."

Riveted, they watched Lee Heist explain his mixed emotions about authorities finding his ex-wife.

"He definitely has no desire to talk to her. I don't blame him, Maude. And look, her daughter said she hopes she rots in hell."

Images of Gigi, Joshua, and Alice wishing her the same fate crowded her mind. Her prank had gone on for months, but she couldn't admit her mistake. What would her family say? What would Ursula think of her?

"Do we have to keep watching this? You seem disturbed, Maude. Looks like you've tuned out completely."

She shrugged. "I don't know. Seems like she was under a great deal of pressure. Raising children, working, and juggling life gets hard. Add a man wanting a divorce and it can be dicey. May I ask you something, Ursula?"

"Go right ahead."

"Do you have any regrets? I mean, about decisions you've made in life."

"A few. I regret not being more forgiving toward my husband. He was a workaholic and I didn't appreciate his sacrifices to make our family comfortable." Ursula surveyed her comfortable digs.

"He made this all possible. I also regret not learning more skills. I've been doing wonderful things since moving back home. My husband left us well off, but I wish I'd learned different things to pass on to my son and grandkids. Keeping up family traditions is a big thing in the South." She paused. "Any regrets on your end?"

Mattie's days in Savannah flashed before her. She couldn't divulge honest regrets since she hadn't been forthcoming with Ursula. "I have lots of regrets. At times I feel like a fraud. Maude the fraud. I can keep a secret 'til Judgment Day, and there are things about myself that make me ashamed."

Ursula chose not to push the matter. She'd give her time to spill her secrets. "I guess I did sound judgmental. I can't understand what would make anyone, especially a mother, leave her children. Then again, I only had one child, a loving husband, and extended family to help me out."

"Life is hard. People like you have it made."

"White people like me?"

"People with support systems like you. My thoughts had nothing to do with race."

Ursula took a deep breath. "Maude, I want to tell you something, but I don't want you to think less of me."

Afraid of what she might say, Mattie asked, "You're not hiding anybody in the backyard, are you?"

"Of course not. You said race wasn't on your mind, but it's on mine."

"Go on."

"Before my finance career, I worked briefly for a fashion magazine in the sixties. During the days of Hermès Kelly bags and expensive lunches, I wrote stories and had photography assignments. A dynamic young lady joined us after a big affirmative action stink. She carried herself with grace and style, came from a well-to-do family, and could turn out copy like no one I'd ever seen. But she was black, and the sentiment was she didn't belong with us. The sandbagging began the moment she arrived. Her stories mysteriously disappeared, and when her stories ran, the editors made her print smaller. Someone poured urine in her coffee. The final straw came when she was given an assignment she couldn't possibly accomplish since she was sent to a country club to cover a story."

"She was denied entry, wasn't she?"

"Not exactly. The gatekeepers assumed she was hired help, so she went with it. It was an amazing story about the event and a spot-on piece about the traditions of the women's group involved.

"When the editor-in-chief read it, he couldn't ignore her talent. However, that story vanished as well. I saw him rip it up and accuse her of not turning it in on time."

"What does this have to do with our conversation?"

"I confronted him about RayAnne and didn't get far. I told him she was so exceptional. He was a good old Southern boy who'd migrated to the North. He looked me dead in my eyes and said, 'She is an exceptional nigger, but she's still a nigger.'

"A vote was taken amongst the staff as to whether she should stay. I was the lone holdout. I felt she should have been given a chance, but her presence made everyone uncomfortable. My job was threatened if I didn't go along with everyone else. The decision had to be unanimous. A tremendous amount of guilt overwhelmed me because I wish I'd done more to help her."

"You did all you could."

"When you said 'we' earlier, meaning black people, I thought of RayAnne and how talented she was. I also wanted you to know that I value you as a person and I didn't befriend you with any ulterior motives."

"Whatever happened to RayAnne?"

"She went on to start her own publication. She did well for herself. I reached out to her once and she never responded."

Mattie eyed the door. "I'm going back down to my place. My stomach's not doing well."

"Did I upset you?"

"No. I need to get some rest. All that grocery shopping and action tuckered me out."

"Let me grab my jacket to walk you back."

"I'll be fine. I need some time to myself."

Ursula linked arms with her friend and walked her to the door. She worked hard at curing her foot-in-mouth disease, but she found herself offending Maude more than comforting her. She couldn't explain it, but the closer they got, the farther away the friendship felt. She would work harder at strengthening their connection.

"Call me if you need anything, Maude."

She nodded and headed home.

31
Our Life Together is Over

Alice swatted Robert's arm and sipped her coffee. "This location is fine. I didn't want to run the risk of someone seeing us."

"We're getting closer. The last sighting of Kenny Graves was in Chattanooga, Tennessee. That's his real name. He has more aliases than the law will allow. If we can get the authorities to close in, we stand a chance of getting the money back."

Nestled in back of Gary's Place, Alice took in the abstract paintings and enjoyed the cozy atmosphere. She'd never heard of the quaint spot in Pooler, but she relaxed as he gave her updates.

"How did you find him?"

"We're not the only congregation he swindled. I've been in touch with several other pastors in Georgia and surrounding states."

"This is still surreal. At this point, I don't care about the money. I want him caught so he doesn't take advantage of anyone else. Several of our members invested their life savings with him."

He cupped her hands. "I have a favor to ask of you."

"What is it?"

"About thirteen of the members are suing me. I want you to get in on the suit with them."

She snatched her hands back. "I can't do that. Our original plan was to track him and get our money back."

"This is how we'll do it. With your name in the suit, it makes our dealings less conspicuous. You'll be another member getting her just due. Since the suit is personal, you'll get money from me in addition to the funds you recoup from Graves in the suit."

"Why would you do that for me?"

"Because you deserve it. You're still with Beryl, aren't you?"

"Yes."

"How is he treating you?"

"We are getting along. He's eased up a lot, but I'm sure it's because of what happened with Davina. I went back home in an attempt to get back at him, but I don't feel the same anymore."

"Davina's gone. She came back to get the rest of her things. Said she needed some time alone."

"I thought you two would work things out."

"If it's meant to be, she'll be back."

The lawsuit came to mind again. "I'd feel low joining the others to sue you. Besides, money can only do so much, and it can't take the place of family."

Alice's sullen face grabbed his attention. "What's wrong? Your emotions are written on your face."

"I miss my family, especially my mother."

He held her hands again. "I'm all ears."

"I'm so lonely. I've never discussed my mother's disappearance with you, but she put stipulations in her will. We're all supposed to be doing things to better ourselves before we get the money. Problem is, we're not really talking to each other right now."

"Why not?"

"They're mad because I went back to Beryl. I never thought I'd miss arguing with Gigi or making fun of Joshua's women, but I do. For a short time, we were bonding after Mama's funeral. Then things changed."

"Your phone still works, doesn't it?"

"Of course."

"Sometimes, you have to make the first move. Doesn't matter who was wrong, or who upset whom, it's good to swallow your pride and make an attempt."

Robert was still holding her hands when Beryl approached their table.

"So this is where you get your eye exams these days?"

"Beryl!" Her anger rose. "You followed me?"

"Don't Beryl me! Get your things and let's go!" He pulled her arm but was shocked by Robert's strength as he removed his hands from her arm.

The men stood face to face now. "I asked her to meet me here. Don't blame her for anything, and don't you dare put your hands on her."

"So we're playing tit-for-tat games?"

"It's nothing like that, Beryl. We're trying to get the money back that was lost through the scheme. She's here trying to get your family's share."

Alice sighed, grateful Robert came to her defense. She ignored the onlookers engrossed in their drama. She also noticed Beryl counting to ten backward, one of the techniques he'd learned since attending anger management classes.

Beryl, unsure of whom to believe, addressed Robert. "You couldn't talk to me man to man?"

"I didn't exactly plan on talking to you at all considering the Davina situation. It's taking everything in me to not do anything to you."

Beryl took a few steps back. "I'm…look, let's just go, Alice."

She grabbed her purse. "I'll be in touch with you, Robert."

Robert watched them leave. Alice wilted with each step she took.

Once outside, Beryl pointed toward his car. "Let's talk."

"I can't leave my car here."

"You won't. I need to say what's on my mind, then I'll leave."

Alice sat in Beryl's car and waited for him to speak.

"I didn't *follow* you as you put it. You didn't answer my calls and I wanted you to know Attorney Durk called the house for you. He said something about handling a personal matter regarding your mother. I noticed you've been moping for months since you came back home. Why did you come back anyway?"

"To get back at you for all the things you did to me! Being stuck under your thumb cost me so many relationships. My mother is dead and I never got a chance to say goodbye to her, I'm distant from my siblings, and I don't have many friends," Alice spat.

"Alice, I treated you badly. I acknowledge my abuse and my temper. If I came home and found you in bed with someone else, I would've murdered you."

"I wouldn't bring another man into our house."

"I know."

"Why are we talking? Why are we even here?"

"Alice, I want a divorce."

His words knocked the wind out of her. "This is about Davina, isn't it?"

"Davina was a one-time mistake. Weakness got the best of me."

"You don't love me anymore?"

"Love isn't the issue. I'm miserable, you're miserable, and we're wasting each other's time. We need to move on."

In all her scheming, she never considered Beryl's stance. They'd gone through the motions so long life without him hadn't occurred to her. At least not with him initiating the move.

"There must be someone else in your life, Beryl. Why the sudden change?"

"Not someone. Something."

"Something?"

"My mother's misery. You didn't travel with me last weekend to visit my parents, but all these years, I never realized how much I'm like my father. I hated the way he treated my mother growing up, but I saw myself in him and you in her. She shuffled around the house taking orders from him, hiding in the bedroom until he told her she could come out. She may as well have been a zombie."

"Your father abused your mother?"

"He didn't hit her, but he ruled her with an iron fist. Her sole purpose was to serve him. If he abused her physically, I never witnessed it."

Alice leaned back in her seat. What would she do now? She'd burned so many bridges she could smell the ashes. Where would she go?

"I *followed* you because I didn't want to move out of the house without talking with you first. I started packing clothes and will get the rest of my things later."

"Why are you moving out? I can stay with Synaria or talk with Joshua about staying with him."

"Alice, you're a grown woman. You made our house a home and it's yours. This divorce won't drag on. We'll split the assets and I'll make sure you're okay. I'm not living this way anymore."

"What about the money from the Ponzi scheme?"

"Keep it. Trust me, I'll be fine."

She should have been thrilled. She'd dreamt of being free from Beryl's spell for so long, but now, fear gripped her. She went from her parents' home to his. How would she pay bills? Buy groceries? She couldn't navigate the world alone.

"Beryl, maybe we should try and work things out."

"This isn't up for debate, Alice. Our life together is over."

32
Reverse Deception

"A little to the left, Synaria."

"If you stop moving, it will be easier."

"But it feels so good; I haven't done this in a long time."

Synaria kneaded Joshua's shoulder blades until they slackened. How a routine wellness check turned into a back massage is anyone's guess, but she was happy he'd stopped by to see her. She noted the stiffness in his body as he spoke and offered to give him a back rub.

"Are you sure you heard her correctly?"

"Josh, Beryl and Alice are getting a divorce."

"He's too evil to walk away from her. Something else is going on."

"If I hadn't seen it for myself, I'd agree with you. I'm telling you, he snatched all his things! Clothes, shoes, golf clubs, everything."

"She let you in the house?"

"Reluctantly."

Joshua wanted to believe what he heard, but they'd been down that road before with Alice. He'd stay as far from the situation as possible.

"When did all this happen?"

"She called me crying last night. I hadn't heard from her and was shocked she reached out to me. I was a bit hesitant to go to the house, but I did."

"And?"

"She was in the middle of the bed crying her eyes out. At first I thought they'd gotten into a fight, but when I realized she was mourning his departure, I wanted to smack her."

"Exactly!"

"Not so fast."

"Why are you defending her again?"

"It takes a long time to break the chains of abuse. The devil you know is more comfortable than the one you don't."

"So you're saying my sister would rather be with a wife beater instead of by herself or with a good man?"

"Until she's safe and healed, yes. Our job is to get her to safety."

"Your job, not ours."

"Ours."

"Not until she apologizes to me."

"Have it your way. I bet if something happened to her, you'd never forgive yourself."

He didn't respond. He still hadn't accepted his mother's death; losing Alice would crush his heart.

"Let's suppose—" His cell phone interrupted his statement. The 770 area code made him tremble. *Deborah.* Joshua removed Synaria's hands from his neck. "Mind if I take this call in another room?"

"Sure." She motioned him toward the patio.

He stepped outside, took a deep breath, then answered.

"Deborah, why haven't you called or responded to my messages?"

Her silence annoyed him. The least she could do was explain herself.

"Deborah—"

"Don't hang up. It's Langston."

Although he was outside, the wind disappeared and his chest constricted. He'd waited for the moment to speak to his son, have a chance to explain himself, but now the words were caught in his throat.

He managed, "How did you get this number?"

"Everything changed when you came to the condo and no one was giving me any answers. I had to find out the truth for myself."

"Do you, I mean, who do you think I am?"

"That's what I came to Savannah to find out."

"You're here?"

"Yes. I'm staying at a Best Western off the Interstate. Mom thinks I'm visiting one of my soccer buddies. I have an idea who you are. I just need confirmation."

"Listen, I'm at a friend's right now, but I'm heading home. Meet me there. 6704 Calypso Road."

"I'll MapQuest it."

"Does Deborah know you found out about me?"

"No. I've named this ride the reverse deception road trip. See you soon."

Joshua ended the call and went back inside. He watched as Synaria busied herself folding clothes on the couch.

"So, is Deborah your latest conquest?"

The question broke his concentration and fear. "What?"

"You said the name Deborah earlier. I assumed she was someone new you were dating."

"We used to date. She's my son's mother."

"Right. Alice told me about her. What's going on? Is she here?"

"She isn't, but my son is."

She placed the pile of towels on the coffee table. Alice had shared Ms. Mattie's covert operation of keeping Langston a secret. "Have a seat."

Joshua rubbed his hands down his pant legs. He'd never so much as babysat, let alone had any paternal instincts. How does a father speak to a son? He leaned back on the sofa.

"Where is he now?"

"He's on his way to my house."

"Get going. He's waited long enough to get to know you. I'll be here if you need to talk."

She practically scooted him out of the door and watched him drive away.

She called out to the Universe. "Please let the meeting go well. Josh needs a little joy in his life."

33
Granny Was A Mess

Months had passed since he'd first laid eyes on Langston, but raw emotions kept him glued near a huge planter in the front yard. Generations of Benson men were nestled in his son's features. High cheekbones, a strong jawline, and dark, seductive eyes were family trademarks. Langston inherited them all. He was handsome, clean-cut, and dressed casually in a Georgia State T-shirt and Levi's. Langston shifted a quilted backpack on his shoulders and closed the gap between them.

Sensing his father's fear, he smiled and asked, "You gonna keep staring or you letting me in this nice house of yours?"

Benson humor, too. "Come inside," was all Joshua could muster.

They sat in the living room as Langston placed the backpack on the love seat. Langston's eyes wandered on family photos placed along the fireplace and on the sofa table. Neither knew what to say, so Joshua took the lead.

"Langston, I'm glad you reached out to me. I'd been trying to introduce myself, but your mother thought it best we wait until the time was right."

"Mom doesn't know I'm here. She always thinks she knows what's best. Things were bad before you showed up; now they've gotten worse."

"What happened?"

He sighed. "I've always felt something was a little off with my family. I've attended the best schools and have great friends, but something was always missing."

"Missing with Ennis or with your mom?"

"Everything. A few days after you left, Mom and Enny C had a big blowout. I stopped by to get a few things and heard them going at it on the patio. He accused her of going behind his back to see you. She denied anything was going on between you two. Since I'm used to them arguing, I was about to walk away when he asked, 'Does he want a paternity test after all these years?'"

Joshua flinched. He took a deep breath and waited for Langston to continue.

"I didn't wait to hear anything else. My life felt like one big lie and I left. Instead of confronting her about what I heard, I investigated. Most of my childhood mementos are still at our Snellville house. Every weekend I'd drive out looking in the garage, the attic, every place I could think of for clues."

"Deborah didn't suspect anything?"

"She works to keep Dad off her mind. She probably didn't notice."

"What led you to me?"

"These." Langston grabbed the backpack from the love seat and removed an oversized box. He slid the box on the coffee table and opened it. Powder and perfume scents filled the space as he removed a stack of letters in Mattie's handwriting.

Joshua picked up a letter. "These are from my mother." The unfamiliar post office box grabbed his attention. What else didn't he know about Mattie Benson?

"From what I read, your mom was a silent partner in my upbringing. These are just a few of the letters I found in a secret space my mother had in the guest bedroom. She sent recipes, gave advice on how to take care of my cuts and bruises, and sprinkled in some relationship tips."

Joshua opened a letter and silently read his mother's pride in him after he snagged a good job. She also nudged Deborah to reach out to him and tell the truth. He slid the letter back in the envelope.

"I wish I had known about you. I could've been a part of your life in some way."

"Grandma Sampson wouldn't allow it. After I found the letters, the way she treated me all made sense. She was never pleased with my grades, never hugged me, never told me she loved me or was proud of me. She got better before she died, but looking at me was like looking at Mom's mistake. Mom wrote a letter to your mother she never mailed. She confessed that about Grandma Lorena."

"Come with me. I want you to see your family."

Langston zeroed in on photos along the mantel. He listened to his father talk about his fabulous aunt, Gabrielle, his shy aunt, Alice, and his grandparents. Each story about Mattie made him laugh.

"Granny was a mess. Sounds like she kept you guys in check."

"She did. I wish we'd done better by her."

"She came to my tenth-grade honors ceremony."

"Come again?"

"Looking at her photo, it clicked for me."

"I'm not following you."

"My grandparents were out of town for something and Dad couldn't be at the ceremony. The woman on this photo"—he pointed to Mattie—"came to congratulate me. Mom pretended she was an elementary teacher of hers. She had lunch with us and told me to keep up the good work."

Joshua felt the sting of her betrayal. There was no reason she should've kept Langston a secret from him.

"Was my father with her?"

"No. She came alone."

They chatted for hours until Langston's stomach growled.

"Let's grab a bite to eat, Langston."

"I haven't eaten since around noon. Seafood would be nice. Everybody's always bragging on Savannah's seafood."

Joshua grabbed his keys, grateful for the second chance he'd been given to know his child. He'd deal with his resentment toward his mother later.

34
What Did You Do?

Lori spotted Gabrielle chatting with a new employee as she radioed Herb.

"I'm swapping shirts for a customer. Be back to my station in ten minutes." She made a beeline toward Gabrielle. Though their backs were turned, she couldn't contain her enthusiasm.

"Looks like somebody finally got rid of that ghetto-fabulous Katisha! I mean, one more run-in with her—"

The ladies heads jerked in unison. Lori gulped, embarrassed by her verbal faux pas. Known as the empress of side-eye glances at Target, she gave direct, probing eye contact to the new employee. She did a triple-take. The woman sported active nails in a soft pink tone and wore a simple gold band on her left ring finger. Black hair was braided in an elegant style that framed her delicate face. No over-the-top lip gloss, fake eyelashes, or neon earrings. Even the lotus flower tattoo had disappeared from her face.

"Katisha." Lori leaned closer. "Katisha?"

Katisha took a deep breath. "Yes, Lori."

"What did you do?"

"With what?"

"Yourself. No offense, but you look so…normal."

Gabrielle stepped in. "Is there something you need, Lori?"

Lori scanned blouses in the department and remembered the items draped over her arm. "I need to swap these for a customer." She spoke to Gabrielle but kept her eyes on Katisha.

"What sizes do you need?" Katisha asked.

"One small, one medium."

Lori pressed the shirts in Katisha's arms and waited for her old attitude to return. Katisha smiled and directed Lori to follow her. She rifled through the rack, pulling two shirts.

"Here you are."

Lori sneered. "Thanks, Katisha." She turned to leave, then retreated. "About what I said earlier."

Gabrielle and Katisha waited.

"I really didn't realize it was you. I shouldn't have said what I said, but let's face it, you were skating on thin ice."

"You said what you meant, Lori."

"I mean, you hadn't been to work in three weeks and I assumed—"

"Assumed or hoped I was fired?"

"Everybody speculated that you…never mind. I have to take these shirts back to customer service."

Gabrielle and Katisha waited until she disappeared.

"Can you believe her?"

"Get used to reactions like Lori's. People hold on to *your* past forever. You may never live your past behavior down amongst the people here, but you can grow and do a better job whether you're at Target or somewhere else."

Katisha embraced Gabrielle. "Thank you so much for helping me. It's my first day back and I feel better. I don't feel so weighted down."

"I see the time off did wonders for you. Herb said he'd give you one last chance because of Kirby. Don't blow it." Gabrielle straightened up several scarves. "How's your mother?"

"Still drinking but not as much. She would die if she knew I told you this, but I think she finally stop pining for my daddy. She's been talking on the phone a lot to some guy named Mack."

"I thought you told me your dad moved on with a younger woman. She was still holding out hope?"

"Sure was. I told her there are other fish in the sea, but she wouldn't listen to me. Dad's remarried and I have a little sister named Grace Louise."

"Grace Louise?"

"He named her after his mother and his wife's mom. I'll bring her in the store on my next off day. I don't get to see her as often as I'd like, but she's a lot of fun to hang out with."

"You have a lot going on."

"Tell me about it." Katisha's name rang out over the intercom. "I'm headed up to customer service. Be right back."

Gabrielle placed the final shipment of jewelry on the accessories racks.

"Gigi, what's new in accessories?"

She didn't turn around but smiled at the sound of Nanette's voice. She never understood why employees ventured into their place of employment on off days, but she loved Nanette's presence. She turned around and was pleasantly surprised to see the gentleman next to her.

"Well, who is this handsome man grinning ear to ear and holding your hand for dear life?" she spoke to Nanette as he blushed at her compliment. She'd heard lots of stories about the love of Nanette's life but hadn't met him face to face.

"Gigi, meet Wendell Tucker. Wendell, this is Gabrielle Benson. This is my work partner in crime I told you about."

"Pleasure to meet you." They shook hands. "Nanette tells me you're quite the social butterfly around here. We might have to snatch you up for our bicycle shop."

"I wouldn't fight it. Anything to boost my income."

Nanette scanned the store. "So who's the new girl I saw walking toward the customer counter? Herb finally grew some balls and let Katisha go, huh?"

"You too?"

"What?"

"That *is* Katisha, Nanette!"

"Good Lord, Ms. Agnes! No it's not!"

"Is too."

"What did she do?"

"New hair, shorter nails. The tattoo on her face was actually a paint-on, so she scrubbed it off. I think she looks attractive."

"Clothes are the easiest thing to change on a person. What about her attitude?"

"She's taking it one day at a time. She'll be fine."

Nanette crinkled her nose. "I'm speechless. I'm walking over to see for myself—"

Wendell gently tugged her arm. "Baby, we have to stay on task."

"Right." She reached inside her hobo bag and produced a white envelope with a sweeping flourish. "Tada!!"

"What's this?"

"Open it up and see."

"You thought enough of me to bring me a wedding invite?"

Gabrielle ripped open the envelope. The blue, yellow, and white invitation with confetti strewn about in the background wasn't exactly what she'd had in mind.

"It's an invite to my mother's retirement party. Or as she likes to call it, her graduation."

"Oh. You told me she was retiring from her social work job at Candler."

"Alva Jean Coles is graduating from all those years of hooking up people with housing, Christmas gifts, and health care referrals. I'm sure my dad will be glad to have her home."

"What should I wear?"

"It's a casual affair, but I'm sure you'll wear something fabulous." She nodded her head toward Wendell. "There's something else."

Wendell cleared his throat. "I'd also like you to meet my uncle."

Her face flushed. "Oh no! No matchmaking. I've sworn off men and don't want to be bothered with a relationship of any kind. No dating, no coffee, nada!"

Nanette piped in. "Come on. He's single, no kids, and he just moved back to Savannah from Alaska."

"If he's so perfect, why is he single?" She turned to Wendell for an answer.

"He never wanted to be married while he was in the military. He saw a lot of his friends divorcing, so he decided to stay single."

"Is this why you asked me to your mom's retirement party?"

"No, Gigi. I asked you to the party because your friendship has made me appreciate my mother even more. All the stories you shared about Ms. Mattie made me realize how blessed I am to have my mother in my life. You've taught me not to take her for granted."

"What I wouldn't give to see my mom again. Ms. Alva Jean sounds like a piece of work, too."

The three of them laughed as Katisha walked back into the area.

"Hi, Nanette."

"Hi, Katisha." She hid the shock of seeing her by digging in her purse.

"I left the last of the items in customer service. I'm stocking shoes after lunch."

Fully recovered from seeing the new Katisha, Nanette said, "Katisha, this is my fiancé, Wendell."

"It's nice to meet you, Wendell." They shook hands.

"Likewise."

"I like your braids. They suit your face." Nanette waited for a sassy retort.

"Thanks for the compliment, Nanette." She smoothed her hands over her head. "I'm going to eat lunch. See you later."

The three of them watched her walk away.

"Honey, if Katisha is changing, I know that dolphins are flying and parrots are living at sea," said Nanette.

35
It Happened So Fast

"This is a good thing, right?" Synaria asked Alice. She reread the letter from Savannah State University, unclear of the source of her friend's sadness.

"It happened so fast."

"You were shy one class. How long did you think it would take?"

"Syn, I don't know. I never imagined my life would change so suddenly. Mama hasn't been dead a year and I feel like I'm free falling."

"How so?"

"Beryl is gone, I'll be able to march and get my degree in December, I have the house, and thanks to Robert, I really don't need the money from the inheritance since the civil suit's been settled. The seventy-five-thousand dollars can hold me until I find a job. If that old snake in the grass is ever found, I'll get more money."

"I'll ask you again. This is a good thing, right?"

The two of them reclined in Alice's king-sized bed gorging on homemade sugar cookies with candied icing, butter almond ice cream, and Reese's Sticks. Since being served with divorce papers and receiving news that she was a candidate for graduation, Alice's emotions whirled faster than a roller coaster. They'd eaten at Elizabeth on Thirty-seventh earlier—Synaria's gift to Alice for finally getting her degree—but Alice only finished a quarter of the Spicy Savannah Red Rice with Georgia Shrimp before breaking down. She wanted to go home, have something sweet to eat, and figure out how the next phase of her life would shake out. She chomped a Reese's Stick and changed the channel to *Being Mary Jane*.

"What am I supposed to do now?"

"Live. Be happy. Find a new man as fine as Stephen Bishop to have a baby with," Synaria said, pointing to the actor.

"Stop making fun of me!" She wiped cookie crumbs from her mouth and broke into a seductive grin as the actor glided across the screen. "He is fine, though."

"Yes. And I'm not making fun of you. I guess I don't understand you."

"What do you mean?"

Synaria moved the empty cookie platter to the nightstand and sat up. "You know I'm not religious, but I do believe in a higher power. We're not smart enough to make all of this possible." She waved her hands in a wide arc.

"And?"

"*And*, my friend, I watched you praying outside the library and some days in the children's area for a way out of your situation."

Her shoulders slumped. "You saw me praying?"

"Crying, too."

"Pathetic Alice. That's what everyone saw."

"I didn't say you were pathetic. My point is, if you were praying and believing, why is it such a shock that things are working in your favor and for your good?"

"Beryl left me without a fuss."

"Isn't it better he left without a fuss instead of you going to a shelter or being buried six feet under?"

She nodded.

"Do you realize the blessing of him not contesting anything?"

"From what I read, divorces can drag on forever."

"Some divorces; not yours."

"Okay. Good point."

"So let me get this straight. You say you serve this mighty God, but He's only real as long as he answers prayers the way you think He should?"

"I didn't say He had to answer things my way."

"You could've fooled me. All I hear is a woman still moping and whining when she should be praise dancing."

"For someone who isn't religious, you sound like an evangelist to me."

"No. I just believe the Universe evens everything out in time. You reap what you sow, and you get what you think you'll have. Somewhere you believed you deserved better and the Universe, or your God, agreed. Take the gift."

"What do I do now?"

"What do you want to do?"

Alice sighed. She'd been dancing to the beat of everyone else's drums so long she didn't have a song of her own. "There are too many things to name."

"Name three."

"You sure?"

"I'm waiting."

"I want a smaller house. This is too big for one person. I want something more intimate where I can entertain guests and have family over without exorbitant gas, water, and electricity bills. Kinda like Mary Jane's house."

"Sell this one. It's in a great neighborhood. Say what you will about Beryl, but he kept the house modern, so you should fetch a pretty penny for it. If the smaller house needs renovating, remember Sabir does renovations. What else?"

"I want to design something. My sewing skills are rusty, but I know if I get back into the swing of things, I could have a small line of clothing, maybe do some alteration work. Before our big falling-out, Joshua let me get my old sewing machine out of the house. Toying with it on the weekends has brought back a lot of good memories. I had no idea so many Simplicity and Butterick patterns were in the garage. Some of those clothes are back in style."

"Name one more."

"I want to get to know me. My likes, dislikes, quirks, idiosyncrasies. On a whim I went to the skating rink two weeks ago and laughed until my eyes watered. Sure, the young'uns were dancing, flipping, and doing tricks above my head, but it was so exhilarating. I've also been bowling. It's scary, but I'm learning new things about myself I didn't know."

"Excellent! Since you've put your desires out in the Universe, you have to work at making them a reality."

"Well, enlightened guru, what about you?"

"What about me?"

"When are you going to ask the Universe to hook you up with Joshua?"

"Please. He's a good friend."

"Sure. Don't think I don't see the way your eyes light up when you're near him or that wide Kool-Aid grin you break into when he's around."

"He's a friend."

"Now who's afraid?"

"I'm not afraid. We've both been burned by love. I don't want to let him down and I don't want him to let me down. You never really know a person until you work with them or live with them. I like the little fantasy we have going on right now."

"Letting each other down is inevitable; getting back up and trying again is what makes the relationship magic. If I'd had that with Beryl, who knows what might have happened."

"But who wants to go into a relationship knowing you'll be exposed."

"It wouldn't be called love if it wasn't set up that way."

"See, you're the guru." She drained the last of her Fanta Mango. "I shouldn't be telling you this, but Joshua met Langston."

"How do you know?"

"I was there when the meet-up took place."

"Deborah finally relented?"

"No way. Benson blood flows through those veins. Langston did some snooping and found Joshua. He went to his house and spent hours catching up. Joshua was over the moon after meeting his son."

Alice fingered Mattie's St. Christopher necklace she'd inherited from the jewelry box. "I am grateful, Syn. I also wish Mama had lived to see us fulfill the desires she had for us. Joshua has at least met his son, Gigi is holding down a job, and I finished school like she wanted me to do. It's so unfair she didn't get to see our progress."

Synaria offered her grandmother's signature comfort line. "She's looking down on you from heaven and smiling."

"Yea, but heaven's not here."

36
Your Eyes And Ears

Dear Ms. Mattie:

This is my last correspondence. Since you haven't responded to my previous messages, I can only assume you've decided to stay where you are. Our agreement was for me to watch your family for a weekend, one month tops. I so hoped you'd return and make amends with your children. I have no desire to turn you in to the authorities; you have to deal with the decision you've made. I would, however, like to give you an update as to what I've witnessed with your children. They are a resilient bunch.

I frequent the Target on Abercorn and see Gabrielle often. She is quite the saleswoman. Her looks don't hurt, either, but she has a genuine concern for her customers. Seems she's moved into a little apartment close to the River Walk.

Joshua's son came to visit him. He is your son's spitting image, only a little lighter. I don't have much more to add about their reunion; I only know they are in touch with each other.

Alice is alone these days. I checked the courts public records and discovered she's been served by her husband, Beryl. She will probably be divorced by the time you receive this letter. She is hanging out with her friend, Synaria, more often. Her wardrobe has improved, and she's smiling more.

The money enclosed is what you paid me. I can't keep this money knowing you are still alive. It makes me feel like a co-conspirator. This has been one of the most exciting assignments I've had in a while. It was like watching nieces or nephews grow and develop.

I pray all is well with you and you are experiencing a measure of peace where you're living. If you should need anything, anything at all, I am a phone call away.

Signed,

Your Eyes and Ears

Mattie's heart swelled at his words. She stuffed the money in her purse, fished her pre-paid cell phone out, and thought of calling Ursula. How would she explain herself? What would be the best course of action in this case? More importantly, what lie could she tell to possibly explain her disappearance?

"They don't want to see me. They've probably split that money up and moved on with their lives."

She tossed the phone in her purse again and covered up with the hand-stitched quilt Ursula's daughter-in-law had given her. *The Price is Right*, hot chocolate, and her afternoon nap would cure her heartache.

37
A Modern-Day Boaz

The crowded elevator area made Gabrielle take the stairs. The lively crowd downstairs paled in comparison to the upstairs action at 10 Downing at Churchill's. People covered every space of the restaurant's balcony. The weather cooperated for Mrs. Coles's retirement party; the eighty-degree temperature was warm enough for the August event, but not too stifling. Georgia heat could beat you down worse than Floyd Mayweather in the summer. She pulled the invitation from her purse and handed it to an attendant at the door.

"Gabrielle Benson, you are at table six. Enjoy the festivities."

She stepped inside the party and saw the continued theme from the invitation. Blue and yellow streamers, balloons, and confetti filled the restaurant. People of various ages chatted, laughed, and talked about Alva Jean. Gabrielle spotted Nanette who waved her over.

"I'm so glad you could make it!" Nanette twirled her around, taking in her beautiful dress. "I knew you'd look stunning."

"I've had this old thing forever." She smoothed the ivory, knee-length Ralph Lauren cocktail dress, a gift from Colton. She opened the matching cream-and-pearl clutch and removed a five-dollar bill. "Do we do this now or later?"

"That was totally optional, but come on over so you can meet her."

Gabrielle snaked her way through the maze of well-wishers until she reached Nanette's mother. An only child, Nanette must have gotten her height from her father since her mother was the epitome of petite. She leaned down and gave her a big hug.

"Mama, this is my friend, Gigi I told you about."

"Congratulations on your retirement!" she shouted over the noisy crowd.

"It's my graduation, Sugah! I've graduated from the school of hard knocks, temperamental bosses, and sometimey coworkers. It wasn't all bad, though. I met some of my best friends at Candler, but I'm ready to step into the next phase of my life. Thirty-two years on one job is nothing to sneeze at!"

"You're right. I pray I can make it the next few years."

"'Net told me you two get on well at Target. I told her to keep rising at the company, but she insists on being an entrepreneur like her father."

"She told me about his businesses."

"I kept the insurance and he kept the good pay flowing. Work well together. Yes we do." She pointed to her husband who held a half-filled champagne flute and laughed with Wendell and a few other men.

Yep, Nanette got her dad's height. Gabrielle eyed the crystal bowl of pins on the souvenir table and swiped a yellow one. "Come a little closer."

"You don't have to tell me twice."

Gabrielle added the five-dollar bill on her dress as the other guests had done. When she was done, Alva touched her bounty.

"I'm putting all this money in our vacation account. First place we're going is Sweden. I've wanted to visit there forever. We normally went to the Caribbean islands and other locales, but never Sweden."

"I'm sure you'll enjoy yourself, Ms. Alva."

"Call me Alva Jean."

"Mama, I'm taking Gigi to her table. Be back soon."

Several men complimented her as she made her way to table six. She smiled, nodded, and kept her eyes straight ahead. Relationship drama was a thing of the past. Ms. Alva Jean was the star of tonight's show.

A handsome man stood when she arrived at the table. He pulled out her chair and introduced himself. "Hello, I'm Peter Tucker. You must be Gabrielle. I'm Wendell's uncle."

She gave Nanette a hard glare before acknowledging him. "It's a pleasure to meet you, Peter."

Nanette disappeared into the crowd before Gabrielle could threaten her. She refocused her attention on her potential beau, taking in everything from his tailored gray business suit, shiny cuff links, starched shirt, and matching blue-and-gray tie. She pretended to drop her purse to get a look at his shoes. Daniel Benson said, "Never trust a man who doesn't take care of his shoes." Peter retrieved her purse, passing the shoe test with flying colors.

"You comfortable with their matchmaking?" he asked.

His grooming matched his looks. His gritty stubble gave him a distinguished air; dark brown eyes flickered with curiosity as he waited for her response.

"I told them I was done with dating."

"So they twisted your arm, too?" he asked. When he laughed at his own question, his gleaming smile put her at ease. Light-brown skin with a smattering of freckles on his cheeks and nose mirrored Wendell's. They could be father and son instead of nephew and uncle.

"So how do you know the Coleses? Through Wendell only?"

"No. Nanette and Wendell are high school sweethearts. We've

known each other's families for years. They're trying to get me to the altar, but they are the ones who need to hurry up and get married. I admire Wendell, though. He doesn't want to get married until he can provide for 'Net in the way he deems appropriate."

"A modern-day Boaz."

"Yes. That's Tucker tradition. You don't take on a wife if you can't provide for her."

She liked the sound of that so much she reconsidered her earlier feelings. Maybe getting to know him wouldn't be so bad. She could use an unattached male friend. Besides, who wanted to keep man sharing with other women? Or men?

Peter glanced at the preset menu. "So what do you think about the party so far?"

"It's obvious Ms. Alva Jean is loved. She must have a thousand dollars pinned to her dress."

"She is a wonderful woman. She and her husband took care of everyone in the neighborhood. Even though she worked, you could count on homemade snacks on the counter and a big pitcher of sweet tea in the fridge after school. She worked the day shift at Candler, so 'Net was never home alone more than an hour after school. I looked out for the younger kids before I left for the military."

Gabrielle felt someone staring at her. Her suspicions were confirmed when she looked two tables ahead. The woman quickly dropped her head.

Her memory raced. She'd dated so many married men in the past she couldn't keep track. Could she be a forgotten wife? Someone with whom she'd had a run-in? She squeezed lemon into her water and took a sip.

"What were you saying?"

"Ms. Alva Jean. She deserves this big night and then some."

"Indeed."

Although others joined table six, Gabrielle and Peter prattled on like old friends. The food, served family style, was passed around the table. Periodically, Alva Jean traveled from table to table urging guests to eat their fill and drink champagne. She beamed with pride.

"The salmon's the best," said Peter.

Feeling eyes upon her again, Gabrielle sipped champagne and looked directly into the woman's eyes. This time, they held their stare.

"Peter, I'm going to the restroom. Be back in a few."

He stood, pulling her chair out again. He watched her walk away. He gave Wendell the thumbs-up as he took his seat.

38
Too Old To Have Children Anyway

She paced the bathroom floor, massaged her temples, and tried to figure out where she'd met the woman. She favored Randy Carter's wife, but he wasn't that old. The woman at the table had to be at least seventy. Maybe it was Randy's mother. With one stall, she knew she couldn't stay holed up in the bathroom long. She'd figure it out; she always did.

She washed her hands, opened the door, and spotted the woman standing near the bar area.

She approached Gabrielle. "Did I startle you?"

"Yes. No. I'm trying to figure out where we know each other from."

"Let's step out on the balcony."

Gabrielle followed her, hands trembling, stomach lurching. She felt a tongue lashing coming on. Probably an admonishment about being a serial adulteress.

"How've you been? I've thought of you all these years and wondered what happened to you."

"I beg your pardon?"

"I wasn't sure whether or not it was you until I scanned the guest list and saw your name. You're just as beautiful now as you were years ago."

"I have no idea who you are."

"You don't know me, but I'm Christin Sweet's grandmother. My name is Lola Roberson."

She stiffened at the mention of Christin's name. It'd been so long since someone said it, she'd forgotten the pain.

She turned to go back inside.

Lola called out to Gabrielle's back. "I'm not here to condemn you. If you give me a chance I can clarify a few things."

"I haven't talked about her for years. I haven't thought about it. I've pushed it out of my mind."

"I'm sure it's painful. I want to tell you something, though."

Gabrielle reluctantly joined Lola on a bench past the pergola. Patrons sipped wine and carried on with their conversations. No one noticed them stroll past.

"You look as if you've seen a ghost. I guess Daniel Benson meant it when he said the incident would be as far as the east is to the west."

Gabrielle remained silent.

"Do you remember anything about Christin?"

Gabrielle nodded. She hesitated, but memories of her old friend came rushing back. "I remember she was funny, smart as a whip, and I could never please her."

"That was my grandbaby. I only visited from New Hampshire twice a year, but I knew she was crazy about you. I never liked the way things turned out, but I'd wished someone would've told you the truth. Might have spared you years of heartache."

"What do you mean?"

"You didn't kill Christin."

"No one believed me. The evidence looked that way, but I swear I didn't do it. My own mother didn't believe me. If Daddy hadn't been in my corner, I..." She dropped her head.

"Those were some troubling days after she passed. I thought I would never get my breath back. The fallout was horrible."

Christin's face flowed through her mind. She pictured them in the basement of the Colonial after they'd just gotten word they'd be bunking in the same cabin at Rock Eagle. The 4-H was one of many extracurricular activities they enjoyed, and her parents spared no expense to make sure the girls had enough clothes and items for the trip. Christin's parents couldn't afford to buy her much; her grandmother paid her camp fee. It wasn't until now she learned her grandmother's name.

"Christin's parents had her later in life. I felt like my daughter should've been satisfied with her husband and her job, but she *had* to have a child. If you ask me, they were too old to have children anyway. Maybe I shouldn't say too old. Cathy had some health issues and having a baby was a big risk. She changed not long after she gave birth. It takes energy to raise a child, and Cathy bit off more than she could chew."

"Was Ms. Cathy depressed or something?"

"We never pinpointed the issue."

"Is that why Christin was at our place all the time?"

"Probably. From what Cathy told me, your parents picked up a lot of her and Purnell's slack. Slowly, I think Christin began to resent you for having such a good family."

"But we took her everywhere and shared everything with her. We did each other's hair. She wore my clothes."

"It's not the same as having your own. You had a little brother and a baby sister. You all had that nice house and hosted parties and teas. You even had the cutest boyfriend in school. Christin was sensitive to all those things."

"I had no idea, Mrs. Roberson."

"You wouldn't have known."

The night of Christin's death came rushing back. They'd headed to the dance at the pavilion from the Calloway building. Her boyfriend, Alaric James, had given her a heads-up that they needed to discuss something. Christin, possessive and clingy that night, wouldn't let Gabrielle leave her side. She finally agreed to dance with a guy from Putnam County, but she kept her eyes on them the whole time.

"Alaric told me she'd been making advances toward him, but I didn't believe him. We were friends and I didn't think she'd do that to me. He told me she'd carved their initials in a tree on the campgrounds. He'd planned to show me later that night. She followed us after we slipped away to talk."

Lola shook her head. "Did she say anything?"

"We were near the water on a small cliff. I couldn't hear everything she said because her speech was slurred, but she kept saying she was better off dead. I tried to grab her hand as she teetered close to the edge of the cliff, but she took two steps back and fell in the water. I didn't know she couldn't swim. We found camp counselors who pulled her from the water. They took her to the hospital, but it was too late."

"I wish she'd known how much we loved her."

"Someone started a rumor that I pushed her. My parents had to come from Savannah to pick me up. There was no press surrounding her death; it would have been bad for the campsite. Everything was hush-hush, but Ms. Cathy insisted that I had something to do with it and begged the police to charge me. I was seventeen, but she wanted me in juvenile detention until I turned eighteen. Even my mother kept asking me if I did it. If my father hadn't stepped in and insisted I be let go, who knows where I'd be now. I had a hard time getting close to girls ever since the incident happened. One of Mama's old friends always said women are each other's competition; always play to win."

"Gabrielle, the reason Cathy backed off of you is because she found Christin's diaries and a suicide note after her funeral. She went to Rock Eagle with no intention of coming back. She took a bunch of her mother's pills with her; they were found in her system when we received the toxicology report. Cathy and Purnell moved out of town after Christin's death."

"I assumed it was because it was hard seeing me still alive."

"I asked her to tell you the truth, but she chose not to."

During restless nights, Gabrielle awakened sweaty, visualizing Christin falling. She wondered if she'd in fact pushed her, that maybe when she advanced a few steps that she'd gotten Christin off-balance. Years of guilt and isolation began to melt away as she took Lola's hands in hers.

"Mrs. Roberson, you have no idea how much this means to me. This is more than a coincidence that you're here."

"I moved here a week after your mother went missing. When I read the story in the paper, I said I'd find a way to reach out to you. You needed to know the truth. I almost came to her funeral, but I didn't think that was an appropriate occasion to tell you what happened."

An understanding passed between them as they faced each other.

"Gabrielle, there you are," said Peter. His steps slowed as he noticed the women having an intimate moment.

"I'll be back in soon, Peter. I'm catching up with an old friend."

They continued to hold hands as Gabrielle sobbed lightly. The tears were needed and cleansing.

39
Probate's Almost Done

Attorney Durk flipped the note over again as he waited for the other siblings. He held it up so Joshua and Langston could read it as well.

"Should I rip it up? I don't want Gigi and Alice to see this," said Joshua.

"Be my guest. I'm sure it's not the only one out there."

"Who would harass a family this way?" Langston noted the care someone took to cut out letters to craft the note. He read it aloud: *"Mattie Benson is still alive. If you give me $15,000, I'll tell you where she is."*

"The least the person could've done was leave a number," Joshua joked.

Durk ripped the letter up and tossed it in the trash can. "You'd be amazed at the number of crazies who scour the obits in search of living relatives to extort. A high-profile story like your mom's was bound to bring out a few vultures and sharks." He added, "When she first went missing, I couldn't keep up with the sightings people reported. A few times, calls came to my phone from a restricted number."

"You do know you can do a reverse lookup and find out who's calling, right?" Langston asked Joshua the question as if everyone knew how phone systems worked. "Grandma Lorena said death always brought out family greed."

Joshua's mind drifted back to their last meeting at Roastfish & Cornbread and Gigi's reaction to Mattie's request. She'd changed her tune since the meeting and he was proud of his sister. In a short time, he'd see how Alice felt about her inheritance. Their estrangement wearied him, and he wouldn't leave the office without trying to make amends.

"Durk, Gabrielle and Alice are here to see you."

"Send them in."

They stood as the sisters walked into the office. They slowed their pace at the sight of Langston.

Unsure of their reaction, Joshua said, "I hope you don't mind him joining us. Whatever's left for me, I want my son to have it."

Gabrielle pushed Joshua out of the way. "Move so I can meet my nephew!"

Langston didn't have time to protest before Gabrielle swept him up in a warm hug. Alice followed suit. They looked him up and down.

"You sure are a good-looking man! I bet you fight the ladies in Atlanta off with a stick!" Gabrielle said.

"Two sticks!" Alice piped in.

He blushed and offered, "I have a girlfriend, but thanks for the compliment."

Gabrielle touched his face and spun him around. "Just like Daddy and Joshua. We have a lifetime to catch up with you. I'm glad you came into our lives."

"So am I."

"Does Deborah know about any of this?" Gabrielle asked.

"Not yet. I plan to tell her this weekend when we go out to dinner. I've been back and forth getting to know Josh, I mean, Dad behind her back."

"Good for you. I'm glad you're getting to know us before something happens," said Alice.

Joshua took a leap of faith. "Alice, it's good to see you."

Robert Crenshaw's words danced in her mind. She'd caused the rift in her family by remaining with Beryl. Squashing bitter feelings was the only option she had.

"It's good to see you too, Josh." She embraced him for a long time. "Excuse us a moment."

Durk chatted with Langston and Gabrielle as they walked to the lobby area.

"I'm sorry for making things difficult between us. Mama and Daddy stayed married, so I thought if I hung in there, things would get better. I only went home to get back at him. That didn't work, either. We were both miserable."

"Alice, you're my sister. Did you think I'd stand by and let someone hurt you? When it seemed you were content in that mess of a marriage, I couldn't take it. I'm sorry for not being more supportive. Synaria has taught me a lot about your circumstances."

I bet she has. Why don't you two stop playing around and get together? "Hard to support a glutton for punishment. I'm not one hundred percent, but I'm getting there. Things won't be healed between the two of us for a while, but I want you to know I never want to be without you in my life again."

"Love you, Sis. Now let's get back in here before Gigi comes out and makes a scene."

"She's calmed down a lot, but let's not push it."

Gigi took stock of them as they entered the room. "I was about to come out after you."

"We know," they said in union.

Durk, proud of the siblings' banter, liked this interaction versus the last time they'd all met. He wanted to address them before his next appointment, so he plowed forward.

"I called you all here today with a few updates and to see how your progress is going. Your mother's will didn't give you all specific ways to achieve her stipulations, but I wanted to know how you're doing with what she asked." He eyed Gabrielle. "How are things going with you, Gigi?"

"I'm gainfully employed. Mama didn't say I had to be anyone's CEO, so I'm working every day and making an honest living. No sponsors." She winked at Alice. "Thanks to Joshua's keen eyes and listening ears, I'm renting an apartment near the River Walk. An exec at Gulfstream had it for use as he came in and out of town. He's relocated and doesn't need it anymore."

"Joshua, how is it going with you?"

He nodded in Langston's direction. "I'm not proud of our reverse deception, but getting to know my son has been great. I wish I knew why he was kept a secret, but I can't do anything about it now. I went back to work two months ago and I'm settling into the reality that Mama's gone."

Everyone cast glances at Alice. She removed a letter from her purse and passed it around.

"It's official. I'm done with school and will be graduating in December." Her voice dropped. "Beryl left me and the divorce will be final soon. I'm putting the house on the market and I'm looking for something smaller." She tried to hold it together, but tears flowed. Attorney Durk passed her a box of Kleenex as Gabrielle massaged her shoulders. "I really don't need the inheritance since receiving money in a civil suit from my former pastor."

Durk reclined in his oversized, leather chair. "Looks like each of you fulfilled your mother's requests. And in a shorter amount of time than I calculated," he added with a grin.

"We did. Mama always said she'd be dead and buried before we all got along," said Gabrielle.

"You can see her again for fifteen-thousand dollars," Langston piped in.

Gabrielle and Alice shot him a crazy look.

"Langston!" said Joshua. He grinned and filled his sisters in on the joke. "Some fool, or fools left a letter here saying Mama's still alive and will tell us where she is if we give them fifteen-thousand dollars."

Alice's shoulders relaxed. "Like when she first went missing and all the people called the TV stations saying they'd spotted her."

"Exactly."

Gabrielle directed her gaze at Durk. "Shall we continue? It's my off day and I have a lunch date."

"Lunch date?" Alice couldn't mask her skepticism. "What's his name?"

"*Her* name is Katisha and her son's name is Kirby. Nanette is also joining us today. I'm hanging out with my coworkers if that's all right with you."

"That sounds wonderful. I don't think I've seen you with a female friend since that girl Christin moved away years ago."

Durk cleared his throat. "Well, the second part of this meeting is a quick update. Luckily, your parents had their affairs in order. Gabrielle entrusted me to assist her with Executor duties in case you two weren't aware. Only a few debts needed to be paid off. I've submitted a final estate accounting, so probate's almost done. The money will be split equally amongst the three of you."

"I thought I wasn't getting anything," said Gabrielle.

"You left before I could tell you Mattie wanted to make sure you all benefited from your father's hard work. She wanted you to know the value of an honest day's pay and have your own money first."

"Durk, I can live with or without the money. Her challenge has made me grow, and I'm grateful."

40
Feels Like I'm Dying

Sharp pain radiated up and down her legs, jolting her from her dream. Mattie tried moving, but the agony rendered her helpless. Her screams filled the bedroom. She tried angling her body toward the dresser, but arthritis made it difficult to grip the mattress. If she could reach the cell phone, she'd be able to call Ursula. She needed her more than ever.

She turned on her back to breathe. She took in short breaths, sat up, and reached for the hand-carved cane Ursula had bought her. Between tears, screams, and curses, she hobbled to the dresser and retrieved her cell phone.

Groggy, Ursula answered on the second ring. "Maude, are you okay?"

"No. Feels like I'm dying. Help me!"

Ursula pulled the covers from her body. "Let me call an ambulance."

"No! Will you please come down here? I can't go to a hospital."

"I'll be right down."

Ursula slipped into a pair of jeans, a hoodie, and Crocs. She made her way to Mattie's cabin and knocked on the door for what seemed like an eternity. Panic-stricken, she paced on the front porch and redialed her number.

"Maude, I can't help you unless you come to the door."

"I can't move."

"I'll have to call nine-one-one then."

She whimpered, "Look under the frog sitting on top of the planter and get my spare key."

Ursula did as instructed. She opened the door and followed her friend's moans and screams to the bedroom. She knelt near Mattie's body, now curled in a fetal position near the dresser.

"It's my legs. I'm having bad cramps. Can you rub them for me?"

"We're getting you to the hospital. I'm not a doctor and I wouldn't forgive myself if something happened to you."

Her leg pains grew sharper as Ursula dialed 9-1-1. Ursula gave the operator Mattie's address and sat on the floor after hanging up.

"I'll get you ready. Where is your coat? You have a light jacket, don't you?"

Mattie pointed toward the closet. The moment she'd feared for the past six months caused shakiness in her limbs. Her heart raced as Ursula rifled through her closet.

"The pink or blue one?"

"Pink."

"Do you have the ICE Blue Button on your phone?"

"A what?"

"It's an app with all your medical information."

Mattie shook her head.

"What about your purse? You'll need insurance and identification. Where is it?"

Mattie's chest tightened. Things were moving too quickly and she grew dizzier.

"I don't like people rambling through my purse!"

"Maude, I'm not—" Ursula remembered their previous conversation and her sensitivity about her past. She didn't want to come across as the great white hope and offend her, so she said, "Tell me where it is. When we get to the hospital, we can let a nurse or social worker go through you things. If necessary, I'll pay the bill for you."

Through the pain, Mattie said, "I can pay my bill. Cash if I have to." Able to flip over on her back again, she said, "Look in that bottom drawer. It's the black purse next to my pistol." She winced and pulled her legs toward her chest.

Ursula imagined wads of cash in her purse. She remembered the day Maude told her she didn't trust banks and cited stories of lenders folding and people losing tons of money. She sighed as the ambulance whirred and came to a halt in front of the cabin. She ran to the front door and led the EMTs to the bedroom. They positioned the stretcher near the bed.

"My name is Whitney. What's going on, Ma'am?" She and her male counterpart lifted Mattie and placed her on the stretcher. Ursula held her hand.

"Leg cramps."

"What's your name?"

Mattie didn't speak.

"Her name is Maude."

Mattie snatched her purse from Ursula and held it to her chest. She decided to suppress her pain in an attempt to make them leave. If she stopped screaming, maybe they'd go. "You not planning on keeping me long, are you?" she asked above a whisper. "If you give me some Advil PM or a sedative, I'll rest here. I don't like hospitals."

"Wouldn't dream of it, Ms. Maude. Terrance and I are here to take care of you. You'll love the team at Habersham. We'll have you back home in no time."

Mattie relented. She'd think of something during the ride along.

"Your name is—"

"Ursula. I'm a friend of Maude's."

"Can you contact her next of kin to tell them we're en route to Habersham?"

"She has no family. I'm all she's got."

"Very well."

"I'll lock up and ride with her."

Ursula locked the door and climbed in back of the ambulance.

"I'm with you, Maude. You don't have anything to worry about."

Tears streamed down Mattie's face as Ursula rubbed her hands.

41
A Case Of Mistaken Identity

Two hours passed as Ursula waited. She swilled the last of her stale coffee and made lines with her nails in the Styrofoam cup. Other family members sat patiently as their relatives were being seen in triage. She walked to the nurse's station.

"Where is your restroom?"

"Just down the hall."

"Thank you."

She used the bathroom and sat next to the same gentleman she'd chatted with earlier. She grabbed a magazine and flipped several pages when a nurse approached her.

"Hi. I'm nurse McArthur. Are you here with—" she eyed the clipboard—"Maude Benefield?"

"Yes."

"How are you related to the patient?"

"We're not related. I'm her neighbor."

"Are any relatives available?"

"No."

"Could you tell me what happened before the ambulance arrived?"

"She called me complaining of leg cramps. I got down to her cabin as fast as I could and called the ambulance. She didn't want to come to the hospital at all."

"That's the general sentiment of our elderly patients."

"Is she going to be okay?"

"Should be. We have her stabilized and she's napping. We'll need you to fill out some forms. Routine procedure. We'll need Mrs. Benefield's insurance information for billing purposes. Any other questions you have can be answered by the attending physician."

Ursula took the clipboard, sinking into her seat. She hadn't been in a hospital since her husband's illness. The smell of commercial antiseptic tickled her nostrils as she got to work on the questions. She aced the top portion of the form with Maude's name and address.

Who thinks to ask friends questions about medications? Family physician? Allergies? Surgeries? She left most of the questions blank. A few of her friends in New York created medical cheat sheets for each other as a cautionary measure. *I should've done the same thing with Maude.*

Nurse McArthur reappeared. "Before I forget, here's Mrs. Benefield's purse. She held on to it for dear life until she fell asleep. You'll probably need it to get her insurance information."

"Thanks so much, Nurse McArthur." She placed it in her lap. "I'm naming this purse Fort Knox. She guards it like a hawk."

Nurse McArthur chuckled. "I bet she's got a million dollars in that thing." She crossed her fingers and gave Ursula a wide grin as she walked away.

She unzipped the purse, admiring its neatness and order. As she guessed, three stacks of bills with paper clips lined the bottom of the purse. She took out the wallet and searched for an insurance card. Maude's impish grin on her license warmed Ursula's heart. Today was her birthday. For the first time since they'd become acquainted, she caught a glimpse of Maude's beautiful dark brown eyes. There were also photos of two women and a man who resembled her friend. Ursula gripped the side of the chair when she read the name *Mattie Benson.*

She searched the area for Nurse McArthur. Perhaps this was

the wrong purse, or a case of mistaken identity. She squeezed her eyes shut and reopened them. Same face. Same smile. Her skin tingled as she flipped through receipts and credit cards. She was gripped with a sudden coldness.

Calm down, Ursula. Calm down.

Still feeling a weird sense of loyalty toward Maude, or Mattie, she concocted a lie and approached the nurse's station again.

"Excuse me," she said in a shaky, disbelieving voice.

The receptionist looked up from the computer screen chomping a huge wad of gum. "Yes."

"Ummm, I've been working with a family trying to find their grandmother. Do you know where I could find out whether a person is missing? Do you have a database of some sort here?"

"We don't. Do you have Internet access?"

"I do."

"If the person is missing, they'll be in the GBI database."

"GBI?"

"Georgia Bureau of Investigation."

"Any other sites?"

"If you have the man or woman's name and they're elderly, look to see if a Mattie's Call was placed." She blew a huge bubble and switched her Bluetooth from her right ear to the left.

Mattie's Call. The irony. "Thank you."

She whipped out her smartphone and plopped down in her chair. Her hands trembled as she accessed the GBI database. Faces of men and women popped up on the screen. She typed in the name "Mattie Benson" with no luck. She switched to Bing and typed in "Mattie Benson." At least a dozen hits crossed the screen. One article titled "Funeral for Mattie Benson held at El Bethel" jumped out at her. She scrolled to an obituary through Legacy.com, clicked on it, and sank deeper in her seat as she read. Not only did Mattie have family members, but she was loved by the community as evidenced in the guest book signatures. She dug in the purse again and found Mattie's phone. She looked through the contacts and found the name "Joshua." She took a deep breath and dialed his number.

42
Stop Playing On The Phone!

Joshua planned the siblings' only affair at their childhood home. Since their last check-in with Durk, they each made a point to contact each other through calls and text messages. They agreed that no more than forty-eight hours would pass between them without some form of communication.

"Think she would've liked this spread?" Alice asked. She scooped potato salad onto the good china Mattie reserved for special occasions.

Gabrielle set slices of the spiral HoneyBaked Ham on a large platter and called over her shoulder, "Only if she had a say in every single piece of food served. She was so picky." She snuck a piece of ham and kept her back turned.

"Smells like you nailed the dressing, Gigi," Joshua said.

With her back still turned, she curtsied. "I do my best to please," she said, chawing the ham.

"Sneaking food like always, huh?" Alice asked.

Joshua decorated the dining room in Mattie's favorite colors, red and blue. The three of them dug out some of her recipes or made her dishes from memory. She believed a good dinner should have one or two meats, three sides, a great homemade drink, and one dessert. She didn't like to go overboard with food.

"Did Langston ever talk to Deborah?" Gabrielle asked.

"Finally. She wasn't thrilled about him getting to know me, but he's a grown man who can make decisions for himself."

"I'm looking forward to him joining us for Thanksgiving," said Alice. "By then I should have the keys to my new house. I'd like to host dinner."

"You?" he asked.

"I've wanted to host dinners, entertain guests, and have barbecues for years."

"We always had the best parties on the block. Our parents never met a stranger and made folks feel welcome. It will be a smooth transition for you, Alice." Gabrielle placed the platter on the table.

"I'm so hungry my stomach is tap dancing. Let's eat," said Joshua.

Joshua led them in prayer as they held hands. The food's aroma filled the room like old times. They hadn't said "Amen" before Gabrielle swiped two yeast rolls from a plate. Joshua chided her but gave her butter.

He passed the scalloped potatoes and asked, "So we're all in agreement about selling the house?"

"We should. No one is living here and I'm not excited about the prospect of being a landlord. Even if a rental company handled it, people don't take care of your things like you do," said Gabrielle.

"What about all the things in here?" Alice poured sweet tea from a pitcher.

Gabrielle's excitement grew. "Yard sale. We could net a small mint from all the clothes, shoes, and household items in here."

"Dad always wanted us to have a place to come home."

"I get that, Josh, but neither of us needs this house." She faced Gabrielle. "Didn't you say this was too much room for you?"

"It is. It's paid for, but the money we'll pay out for taxes and insurance could be used for other things. I don't need this much space."

"Another thing we need to consider is—"

His cell phone interrupted his comment.

"Thought you turned the ringer off," said Alice. She playfully rolled her eyes at him. She hadn't gotten used to having a phone in the dining room or at dinnertime. One more lingering effect from the Beryl days she would conquer. "At least take it off the table. Those things are appendages."

"I keep it handy for work or if Langston needs me."

"Synaria too?" Gabrielle teased.

He ignored her question and silenced the phone. "I don't recognize the number anyway."

"Don't think I'm dropping the Synaria subject. I think you two would make a good couple if you stop joking around."

"Oh, you can pry in my personal life but won't tell me who you were with at the park last week?"

"Gigi was with someone?" Alice asked.

"Some light-skinned guy with freckles. By the time I made my way to her, they were gone."

"Peter is a friend. I got off work early and we had a sandwich. Simple as that, Josh."

"So you say."

The phone vibrated again.

"Maybe I should get this. Some desperate soul is calling back to back."

He answered the phone, then abruptly ended the call.

"Who was that, Josh?" Alice asked.

He rubbed his hands and took a long swig of sweet tea. "I'm not dealing with any crazies tonight."

"What?" Gabrielle's hands shook.

"It's some crazy wo—"

The phone vibrated. This time he swiped it from the sideboard and put it on speaker.

"Hello?" The distant, unfamiliar voice sounded desperate.

"Who is this? Why are you harassing us?"

"Don't hang up again. My name is Ursula Kinsey and I'm at the Habersham Medical Center with your mother, Mattie Benson."

Gabrielle dropped her fork; Alice's eyes widened.

"Listen, lady, I don't know who you are, but you need to stop playing on the phone! How did you get my number anyway?"

"You don't understand. I found your number in her purse after she got sick earlier. I befriended her several months ago and thought her name was Maude Benefield. I'm here at the hospital and don't want to cause a commotion, but your mother is still alive."

"We had her funeral months ago."

"I read the obituary. I also read about the Mattie's Call. She's still alive. We're at the hospital because she was having leg cramps."

Alice scooted closer to the phone. Something about the stranger on the other end made her believe her mother was still in the land of the living. Karen from Grand Oak had told her about Mattie's leg cramps. She'd intended to send her to a doctor, but Beryl told her they couldn't afford it. "If you found her purse, what's inside?"

"Normal things along with wads of money attached with paper-clips."

"That's Mama," they said in unison.

"Have you told anyone it's her?" he asked.

She thought of Mattie's response to Brenda Heist. "No. Authorities and the media would have a field day. She deserves a chance to explain herself."

"We'll be there as fast as we can."

43
What Would People Say?

Gabrielle and Joshua took turns driving to Helen. Alice's shaky hands and teary state forced her in the backseat. Her whininess wasn't helping the situation.

"How many times have I watched people disappear on television and criticize them when they return?" Gabrielle asked.

"No one knew who she was by looking at her? That Mattie's Call went out everywhere."

"Josh, forget about the Mattie's Call. Our mother has been alive all these months and didn't say anything. Anything!" Alice hugged herself in the backseat. She vacillated between anger and relief. She'd have another chance to show her mother how much she loved her, but how much did their mom care about them?

"We can't take a dead woman back to Savannah. What would people say if we show back up with her after all this time?" Gabrielle gave Joshua a quick glance before refocusing on the highway.

"Gigi, Durk will have to help us spin the story. I can't imagine all the legal ramifications of this. How did she get all the way to Helen anyway?" Joshua's phone rang again.

"Joshua, this is Ursula. The doctors have given your mother a mild sedative for the leg pain. They said she'll be out for a while and she has no idea you all are on the way. I'll need a ride home since I came in the ambulance with her. I also need to go back to her cabin to get a few things. Can you pick me up?"

"Did you say her cabin?"

"Yes, she has a cabin. I feel stupid repeating things she's told me, but she said it's been in the family for years."

"What's the address?"

"Fourteen Randall Road. Our cabins are the only three back there. Habersham is in Demorest. I'll be in the emergency room area waiting for you."

Joshua fell silent. He cracked his knuckles and stared out the window.

Alice scooted forward in the backseat. "What did she say? You're acting like Mama's dead." Alice covered her mouth with her hands when she realized what she'd said.

"Not dead, Alice. More like a complete stranger. She kept Langston a secret all those years; now this Ursula woman is saying she has a cabin."

Gabrielle weaved slightly. "You're telling me our parents had a cabin and made us camp out in the woods during the summers?"

"There's no telling what else we don't know about her. Or them." Alice removed a pillbox from her purse. She guzzled water from the gallon jug she always carried after popping two Tylenol. "I'm so nervous I can't talk anymore. Wake me up when we get to the hospital."

They arrived at Habersham faster than expected. Gabrielle parked after dropping off Joshua and Alice near the emergency room. The three of them walked inside as Ursula waved them over. Since there was safety in numbers, they'd do what was necessary if the call proved to be a hoax. Three outnumbered one.

Her uncertain steps made the meet-up slower. She scanned the lobby area as if others were waiting to hear her secret. She brought a shaky hand to her forehead. "I'm Ursula. I'm sorry to bring you out this way. I didn't know what else to do."

Joshua became the family spokesperson. "With all due respect, we need to see our mother first. We've been harassed by people with false sightings."

"I understand completely. She's been admitted to a room on the first floor. Follow me. Visiting hours are over, but I told them her children would be here to visit. They know her as Maude Benefield, so let's keep it going."

They took the stairs instead of the elevator, each wanting to believe they had the chance to make amends with their mom.

"What do we say?" Alice asked.

"Nothing. She's out for at least six hours. Get a look at her and let's go. I want her to be awake when she sees you," said Ursula. She opened the door and waited for the nurse to finish adjusting the IV.

The nurse faced them as they stood alongside the bed.

"Nurse, these are Mrs. Benefield's children. We know we can't stay, but they wanted to see her."

"That's fine. I'm so happy you're here. She was crying earlier over her leg pain and saying she wished her children could help her."

Alice leaned on Joshua's shoulders and sobbed lightly. Gabrielle held their baby sister's hand.

"We have to make this thing right with Mama."

"We will, Alice. I promise you we will," he said.

44
A Whole Other Life

"This is hard to process," said Gabrielle.

"Gigi, you're the oldest. You had no idea this place existed?" Alice asked.

Ursula left them alone in the cabin with the promise they'd meet up in an hour. The cabin, neat and homey, was welcoming and decorated similar to their childhood home. Although she had no family photos in the living room, they found a treasure trove of items in her bedroom closet, underneath the bed, and in her chest of drawers.

"Look at this," said Gabrielle.

She showed her siblings a photo of Daniel and Mattie standing outside the cabin. They were hugged up, younger, vibrant eyes shining. She flipped it over and read, "*We did it, Baby. This is for me and you only. Our escape.*"

Joshua stared at his father. "He never stopped loving her and wanting to please her. I could never live up to that in a relationship."

"You're supposed to have your own relationship. Theirs was a good model, but you have to create your own marriage," said Alice.

Gigi found more photos. "Where were we when they came here?"

"They were really young on these pictures, so I'm guessing we weren't born. In their later years, they probably came here when we stayed with Grandma and Grandpa." Joshua handed the photo back to Gabrielle and opened a bottom drawer of the heavy chifforobe. Letters with the name "Boris Camden, PI," in the return address caught his attention. He removed them and informed his sisters, "I'm going to the living room. Be back in a few."

He kicked his feet up on the coffee table and read the letters that had been opened. Pangs of guilt hit him when he thought back to his mother pleading with him to start the rotation again. He'd put his plan in motion for her to move in, but he'd been too slow. A light tap on the front door interrupted him. "Come in."

Ursula walked in with a reusable shopping bag and sat across from him. "Are you all ready to go back to the hospital? I brought a few things I know she enjoys. We took turns with crossword puzzles. She'd do the top half; I'd complete the bottom." She held up a large print puzzle book.

"She did the same thing with my father." He wrapped the bow around the letters again. "How did you get to know my mother?"

"I saw her coming and going and figured she needed assistance. She was shrouded in those dark shades and running inside before I could get her attention. She was determined to keep to herself, but we're isolated back here. Neighbors should get to know each other."

"Thank you for looking out for her."

"She always said she was alone in the world, but I didn't believe her. The way she nurtured her plants and cared for her home was an indicator of motherly love. I wished she'd opened up to me."

"You would've turned her in."

"No I wouldn't. I would find any living relatives she had. I knew something was going on because she could be jittery at times."

Alice and Gabrielle joined them in the living room.

"Mama has a safe with money and jewelry in there, Josh," said Alice. "She kept the combination in back of it."

"And she has concert stubs, playbills, all kinds of entertainment mementos." Gabrielle held up stubs from a 1972 Bill Withers concert.

"It's like our parents lived a whole other life," said Josh.

"Keeps the spice going," said Ursula. She eyed her watch. "Let's get back to the hospital. This reunion has been long overdue."

45
We Can't Start Over

Mattie's chest rose and fell. The potent sedative made it hard to open her eyes. The hospital bed was no match for her soft mattress; she had to get up and go back to the cabin. She tried turning on her side when familiar voices called out to her, "Be careful, Mama."

She shook off the sound. "Can't be." Her left eye sprang open. She scanned the room and pulled the covers closer at the sight of her children. "What are you all doing here?"

They'd made a pact to stay calm and let her explain herself.

"Ms. Ursula called us, Mama," said Joshua. "I can't imagine a mother of mine being alive and not reaching out to me or us."

"Believe it." Mattie's eyes were open now. She turned away from them and looked out the window.

Gabrielle swallowed hard. "You were disoriented and got lost? Right, Mama. You didn't know what to do, stayed away because you were afraid?"

Her attention stayed focused on the birds outside the window as she spoke. "Thanks a lot, Ursula. I'm sure you're responsible for this mess." Her sarcastic tone bristled them.

"Would you rather I had called the authorities, *Mattie?*"

"The police care more for me than my own children."

"Mama, you know that's not true," said Alice. She reached for her mother's hands, but Mattie folded them as if in funeral repose.

She turned her eyes on them and glared. "It took the three of you thinking I was dead to be in the same place at one time. When I was still alive, how often did you see about me?"

Their silence was her answer.

"All those times I asked you to come to Grand Oak to visit, you were always so busy. Alice, you were locked up with that bossy husband of yours. Gigi, I don't want to talk about whose husband you were with because I never knew, and Joshua, your job may as well have been your wife."

Joshua turned to Ursula. "May we have a moment alone?" She left the room and Joshua began his tirade. "We may not have been the best at taking care of your needs, but at least we didn't keep a million secrets. You kept my son from me!"

"Don't raise your voice at me! Deborah asked me not to tell and I didn't. A woman has a right to choose if she doesn't want a man in her child's life. Even if that man is a biological father."

"But you got to know him in secret. Do you know how that makes me feel?"

"Don't you know him now?"

"That's not the point."

"Seems my leaving made a lot of good things come to pass, so that is the point."

"Mama, I'm going to pretend you aren't saying you left on purpose."

"Alice, you have no reason to pretend. If my going away got you away from Beryl, it was worth it. You look good. You're wearing makeup and you have on decent clothes. Did you finish with your class?"

She waited an eternity to answer. "Yes, Ma'am."

"So you have a degree?"

She nodded.

"Gigi, where are you living now?"

"I have an apartment downtown."

"You paying the rent?"

"Of course."

"Don't 'of course' me. Your financial life was sketchy. I prayed you'd stop getting by on your looks."

Joshua kept an even tone this time. "I read the letters from the P.I. Why are you asking us these questions when you know the answers?"

"I wanted you all to hear yourselves. You went on without me. You actually seemed to be doing well without me."

"But I missed you so much, Mama," said Alice. The fragile member of the trio, she sat on the bed and leaned on Mattie's chest. "Things happened and I wanted your input. It wasn't the same without you around." She practically melted when her mother patted her back.

Gabrielle sat on the opposite side of the bed. "Mama, I'm sorry for being so mean to you. I never forgave you for not taking my side in Christin's death."

"Gigi, I wasn't at Rock Eagle with you. I've always told you all I'm not the kind of parent who upholds her children in everything. I've seen children do some ugly things and the parents will act like their children are as right as rain. Your father and Attorney Durk made sure nothing happened to you. You would never tell me exactly what happened, so I didn't know who was telling the truth."

"You said Christin moved away, Gigi." Joshua was about to fire off more questions, then stopped. "Mama, how do we start over?"

"We can't start over 'cause nobody can go back in time. We can try to do things different, though. I was wrong for what I did to you all. I paid Agatha's grandson, BoPeep, three thousand dollars to bring me up here. Truth be told, I'm shocked he didn't go to the news reporters after I disappeared. I was supposed to be missing until that Tuesday to see what you all would do. BoPeep never came back and I was too afraid to call you all. Me and your daddy have had this cabin for years. I was gonna sit up in these mountains until I figured it all out. Time just got away from me.

"I'm also surprised Boris never got caught spying on you all. He even gave me my money back when I didn't respond to him. If we want to make things right, let's talk about how I'm getting back home. Lord knows I don't want anyone to faint dead away if they see me."

"I called Durk this morning. We'll hash out a good story to satisfy the press. He's a master spin artist, so that's the least of my worries. He said he would stop the will proceedings through probate." For the first time since they'd returned to the hospital, Joshua smiled at his mother.

"Now, I need you all to step out so I can talk to Ursula alone. Have her come back in here."

46
Epilogue: One Year Later

Alice's nerves were on edge as the last of the guests arrived. The weather cooperated for the patio shindig. Mattie sat in a decorated chair at the gift table and directed traffic her way. When someone handed her a box, she rearranged the gifts and gave a warm thank-you.

Katisha and Nanette unwrapped the fruit and vegetable trays and lit candles underneath chafing dishes filled with meatballs and wings. Ladies mingled and laughed as they took in their surroundings.

"Alice, your house looks like something out of a magazine," said Zola, one of Synaria's childhood friends. "Who decorated it?"

"I did most of it myself. I got a lot of ideas from magazines and books. The actual rehab and upgrades were done by a friend of mine named Sabir."

"Honey, you missed your calling as an interior designer. This place is fabulous."

"Thanks, Zola."

Alice had moved in less than a month ago. She had prepared for her round of the rotation by outfitting Mattie's bedroom with her favorite photos, puzzles, and sewing patterns. Four months of hosting her mother excited and simultaneously frightened her. She spared no expense as Robert made good on his promise that she'd get money back from the Ponzi scheme. That money, in addition to proceeds from the sale of her old home and alimony from Beryl, allowed her to breathe and work on her clothing design and alteration business. She hadn't ironed out all the details yet, but she took advantage of local business initiatives created for entrepreneurs.

Mattie flagged Gabrielle as she walked past. "Gigi, bring me a glass of lemonade, please."

"What else would you like, Mama?"

"One of those pimento cheese things."

"Pinwheels, Mama."

"You know what I mean."

Alice joined her mother at the gift table. "I'm going to have the guests eat soon."

"I'm so proud of you, Baby. You started over and you survived."

"One day at a time, remember?"

"I said what I meant and I meant what I said."

They chuckled as ladies lined up at the food table.

Mattie tsked after getting her plate. "Gigi, I didn't think you'd ever make it back. I'm starving."

"I was only gone a minute." She'd spotted Synaria by the pool chatting up ladies from the library. Several of them held her hand as they admired her ring. "It will be good having a new sister. It took Josh forever to propose."

Mattie nodded. "I bet he's not gonna run away this time. He really loves her. I can't say I felt that way about the others."

"The three of us agree on something!" Alice did a victory dance and stopped when Mattie shot a look of disapproval. "What?"

"Stop clowning like that about your brother. He needed to find the right one."

"Whatever you say, Mama."

Synaria came up behind Alice and gave her a big hug. "I'm over the moon that the first party at your new place is my bridal shower."

"You were going to be part of the family one way or the other."

"If it hadn't been for you and Gigi making me open my eyes and my heart again, Josh may have slipped through my fingers."

"After Mama left and we had a long talk, we realized Josh was afraid he couldn't live up to Daddy's example. You broke through those fears, Syn. You'll make a great wife," said Alice.

Synaria laughed, ate, chatted, and played games with everyone. She sat in the center of the women donning a burgundy caftan and a sparkly tiara as she opened gifts. She oohed and aahed at the wide array of presents. She received everything from lingerie, sex toys, cookbooks, and gift cards from various retailers.

She got to the last gift and held it up. "This one doesn't have a card."

Mattie beamed. "It's from me. Had to get my daughter-in-law something special."

Synaria ripped paper from the slim box and pulled an envelope from it. She took a deep breath as she looked at its contents.

"I can't take this, Ms. Mattie."

"Too late. You two own it now."

As she had done with the other gifts, she held it up for her family members and friends to inspect.

Mattie sat back, pleased Durk had helped her gift the cabin to Joshua and Synaria. Daniel had bought the land and had the cabin built four years after they married. They promised each other their marriage would be different than the ones they saw growing up. He'd fulfilled so many promises. He was gone now. She only hoped his son, his seed, would make a good husband and make time for his wife as his father had for her. She planned to be around a long time to witness the continued growth of all her children.

About the Author

Stacy Campbell is the author of *Dream Girl Awakened, Forgive Me* and *Wouldn't Change a Thing.* She was born and raised in Sparta, Georgia, where she spent summers on her family's front porch listening to the animated tales of her older relatives. She lives with her family in Indianapolis, Indiana.

You may visit the author: www.stacyloveswriting.com, georgia peach2814@aol.com, www.facebook.com/stacy.campbell.376, and www.twitter.com/stacycampbell20

Author's Note

Two incidents prompted *Mattie's Call*: A real life Mattie's Call and the wild stories of my nursing home friends. Several years ago, my now deceased sister-in-law walked out of a facility in Atlanta and a Mattie's Call was issued. There'd been a holiday program and she walked out with the choir. We were nervous until they found her. She went back to the facility unharmed, but I never shook the feeling of not being able to tell her how much I loved her and what she meant to me if she had died. I also volunteer at a local nursing home and the stories the men and women share are amazing. One grand diva still talks about the cabin she and her husband bought and kept secret from their children for over forty years. It was their retreat, their place to get away and reclaim peace and quiet.

My siblings and I were fortunate to have parents who loved us and stayed married forty-eight years. In return, we all rallied together in their last days to take care of them. Both my parents died in my sister, Becky's, house. My nursing home friends tell me it doesn't always work out that way. Some of them are lonely, are the last living children of their bloodline, or have estranged relationships with their children. I set out to spread a message of parental love with this work.

Ten million thanks go to Sara, Zane, and Charmaine, for giving me extra time to complete this book. Fear and the reality of writing got the better of me, but I'm grateful they allowed me to finish what I started.

To the lovely book ambassadors and fellow authors who keep inspiring me: Devetrice Conyers-Hinton, Andrea Allen, Jerine Campbell, Author Cathy Jo, Author Renee Swindle Tiffany Tyler, Orsayor Simmons, Deborah Owsley, Ben Burgess, Jr., Julia Blues, Kimyatta Walker, Yolanda Gore, Lasheera Lee, Ella Curry, Tumika Cain, Cyress Webb, Johnathan Royal, Adrienne Thompson, Trice Hickman, Victoria Christopher Murray, King Brooks, Christina Lattimore, Charles Frazier, Alvin Horn, Nhat Crawford, Christine Pauls, Sadeqa Johnson, Victor Carroll, Tressia Gibbs, Curtis Bunn, Sherrod Tunstall, Tammi Kinchlow, Dawn Jones, Teresa Beasley, A'ndrea Wilson, Kiera J. Northington, Anthony Lamarr White, Kim Knight, Christine Pauls and Donna Meredith.

To every book club, radio outlet, public library, Facebook and Twitter friends, hometown squad, and reader who has encouraged me with kindness, food, constructive feedback, and a good old-fashioned, "Girl, that book made my day," I thank you. It is because of you that I strive to be a better writer and master the craft.

To my siblings, I couldn't have asked for a better tribe, and we couldn't have been given better parents. I love you.

IF YOU ENJOYED "MATTIE'S CALL," BE SURE TO CHECK OUT

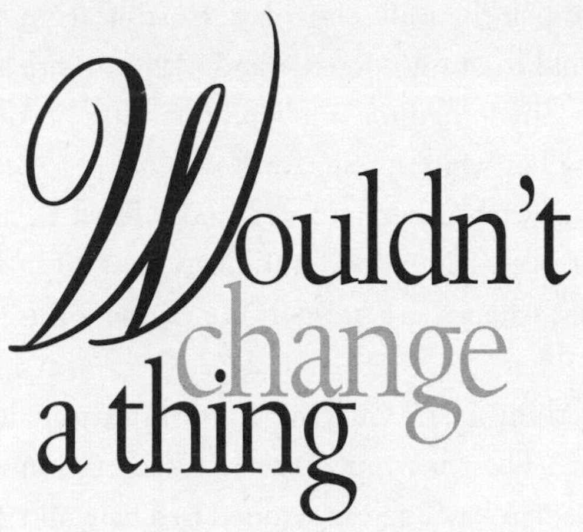

BY STACY CAMPBELL
AVAILABLE FROM STREBOR BOOKS

Then

"Let's face it; everyone in life is passing for something."
—Woodrow Guill, Sparta, Georgia

Clayton Kenneth Myles is my father. That's my story and I'm sticking to it. Well, Clay and his partner, Russell Morris. They are two of many factors that always made me the odd girl. The one with two dads. The one with the rickety family tree.

Clayton whisked me to Atlanta on my ninth birthday; April Fool's

Day in 1984. I'd made a yellow cake in my Easy Bake oven, and before I could lick the milk chocolate frosting from my fingers, Aunt Mavis told me to go outside and play in a tire swing until my ride came. She joined me a few minutes later in the opposite swing, wearing her white nurse's uniform.

We smiled at each other and she said, "Hard decisions have deep consequences." She stood and gave me a tight hug. "This will make sense when you get older. We're doing this because we love you."

A speeding, shiny, black Chrysler Laser interrupted my "What do you mean?" The car topped the hill with a plume of smoky dust chasing its fender. The car skidded to a halt, and out jumped Cousin Clayton, a high school English teacher and the family grammarian. Tall, pencil-thin, and rubbing an immaculate goatee, he looked at us, his dark eyes misty from crying.

"Honey, have you heard the news?" he asked Mavis.

"What's wrong?"

"Cousin, Marvin Gaye is dead! His father shot him in the chest earlier today. The grapevine—no pun intended—is saying he was strung out on cocaine and spending hours watching porn videos in his bedroom. He was wearing a maroon bathrobe he'd had on for days. He was convinced someone was going to kill him. I told Russell something wasn't right when we went to Marvin's last concert, but he wouldn't confirm or deny anything," said Clayton, peppering the rehash with sweeping hand gestures. His purple, short-sleeved cotton dress shirt and tie were soaked, as if he'd run a marathon, and his black slacks were equally wet. Clayton and Georgia heat were archenemies.

"Oh my," said Mavis, clutching her chest. "What a waste of talent. I bet Russ and the other sound engineers are devastated. I know how you love your entertainers and how much you love Russ's studio stories." She gave him a suspicious gaze. "Do you remember the terms of our agreement?"

He eyed me swinging. Her words had jolted him back to the purpose of his visit, his mission. "We have her room decorated in pink and white." To me, he said, "You're going to love your canopy bed and dolls. I found some beautiful dolls on my last trip to India. It makes no sense for a little black girl to be in love with those hideous, pug-faced Cabbage Patch Kids."

Mavis grabbed Clayton's arm and they walked near the hydrangeas. I eavesdropped, caught fragmented utterances floating in the air. Georgia Mental Hospital. Paranoid Schizophrenia. Mall episode. Long recovery. As they leaned into each other, they stole glances at me and shook their heads in pity.

Mama was home one day, gone the next. I knew she wasn't dead. Death always ushered in visitors, fried chicken, potato salad, and a slew of relatives who only appeared for funerals or when spoils were divided.

"Toni, go inside and get your suitcase," said Aunt Mavis. "You're going to Atlanta to stay with Cousin Clayton a few months. You'll be back in time for school in September."

"What about my classes?"

"Clayton pulled some strings. You'll be in a magnet school until June."

I peeled my body from the swing and ran to my room. My jelly shoes squeaked and a small breeze lifted my sundress. I zipped my packed suitcase and thought of my older sister, Willa. Last year, Mama sent her to live with our aunts, Norlyza and Carrie Bell. After making me test the food Willa prepared, Mama said she was poisoning our food with arsenic and d-CON pellets. I stepped onto the porch, suitcase in my left hand, Dream Skater doll in my right. I tiptoed into the middle of the adults' conversation.

Clayton looked at Mavis. "So when is Greta coming home?"

"It'll be a while. Raymond and I have to nurse her back to health again. We can't keep her at the house, so she's at the hospital. She's flushing her meds down the toilet."

"Do you think the episode had something to do with the divorce?"

"Hard to say. You know Greta has blue genes," said Mavis, winking at Clayton.

"Blue genes, indeed," he said.

"Mama has lots of blue jeans," I added. "I want the picture of her in the tank top and Lee jeans. I loved the checkered dress I wore. Daddy was grinning and Mama had that half-smile on her face. I sat between them on the motorcycle in that picture. Remember, Aunt Mavis?"

"How could I forget? That particular cookout is one of the happiest recollections of my brother before he…" Her voice trailed off with the memory.

"What a cute suitcase," said Clayton, lightening the mood. I followed him as he placed it in the backseat.

Aunt Mavis tightened my ponytail holder and hugged me again as I sat in the car. She closed my door and made Clayton promise to call her when we arrived in Atlanta. Clayton pulled down a pair of Ray-Bans from his sun visor. I caressed Dream Skater's hair.

"You ready, Antoinette?"

"Yes, sir. I'm ready."

"Don't be nervous. This is temporary until your mother gets better. You're with family, so there's nothing to fear."

"I'm not scared. I'm excited."

"That's the spirit."

He slid a bubble wrap container in my lap.

"What is this?" I opened the container and flipped the cassette tape over twice. It read *UNRELEASED*.

"Our little secret. Russ smuggled this out of the studio. Sent it two weeks ago when he was out in L.A. doing studio work on Marvin's latest album. Personally, I don't think this little ditty will see the light of day now that he's gone, but we get to hear it before the rest of the world."

With that, he plopped in a cassette and we drove away listening to Marvin Gaye extol the sanctified lady saving her thing for Jesus. We became a dynamic duo that day, Wonder Twins passing for straight and sane, heading to Atlanta munching honey-roasted peanuts and drinking ice-cold Coca-Colas.

Now

"Every morning I wake up clothed and in my right mind, I feel all right."
—Lillian Stanton, Sparta, Georgia

Chapter 1

Threes. It always comes in threes. How else can I explain my fiancé, Lamonte, knocking on my backdoor, my cell ringing repeatedly, and a slew of reporters standing on my front lawn at seven in the morning? I'm not cut out for this. Not on a regular day and certainly not the morning of my engagement party.

"Baby, let me in," says Lamonte.

His voice is so sexy he can talk the habit off a nun. I crack the backdoor open and my heart melts when I see him. During the spring and summer months, Lamonte ditches his suits in favor of starched collared shirts, chinos, and spit-shined oxfords. He holds my gaze, not showing any emotion.

"Lamonte, please tell me what's going on," I demand. I motion for him to come to the patio as I slide the door open.

"You haven't said anything, have you?"

"Said anything about what? Is there something you haven't told me? Is this about the Midtown project?"

Lamonte takes my left hand. I follow him, all towering six feet four inches of him, and sit on his lap at his favorite table in my house in the breakfast nook. We'd picked this one out together on a trip to St. Simons Island last year.

"Toni, baby," he says, rubbing my left hand and massaging my right shoulder. "This has nothing to do with me. It's about you. Actually, your family."

"Is Clay in trouble?"

"I think you should take a look for yourself, Toni."

I take a seat across from him now as he unfolds the *Atlanta Journal-Constitution.* There I am on the front page beneath the caption, "Mother Longs for Reunion with Daughters." Not only does the caption knock the wind out of me, but the accompanying photo leaves me momentarily speechless. It is a replica of the one I keep tucked in the bottom drawer of my home office desk. My sister, Willa, and I wear matching pink and black turtleneck sweaters. Mama had jumped up from her spot next to Willa and me at Olan Mills Studio that afternoon. She refused to pose with us when the photo was taken; she said the people in the camera lens were making fun of her.

Lamonte moves closer now, knowing I have to take in every word, examine the train wreck the *AJC* has created on what is supposed to be one of the most memorable days of my life. He waits for my full explanation. I can't offer one right now. His phone rings, startling us.

"Take it in the living room," I whisper.

I continue reading, thankful I closed my shades last night. Even in this dimness, I feel naked. I look at the photo again and my heart aches for my mother.

Lamonte returns to comfort me again.

He sits back and rubs his clean-shaven face. "That was Richard on the phone. He said the paper will issue a formal apology to you by noon today. The picture was supposed to be in silhouette, but went to print with full exposure. Don't panic, baby. Not now. We'll get through this together."

Richard Phelps, our mutual attorney, pokes fun at people so much we call it his side hustle.

"That's easy for you to say. The *AJC*'s readership and my colleagues all think I'm a garden variety fruitcake." I pause. "Did you say 'together'? As in, we'll go through with this engagement party and wedding?"

"Toni, I made a commitment to you. This doesn't look good, but I want to give you a chance to respond to what I read this morning." He holds up the article.

"How am I supposed to respond?"

"Start by telling me the truth. Please."

"Lamonte, Clay has the answer for everything. But you and I both know he's in no position to answer right now."

He motions for me to sit in his lap again and I enjoy resting there for a brief moment. I feel like a fraud in his arms. I'm trying to find the right words to justify my lies, but I can't. This wasn't a white lie; this was more like a pastel one, the kind you tell when you know the truth will get in the way of your happiness.

"Toni, this is awkward. I'll cook while we strategize."

In Lamonte Dunlap fashion, he goes to the kitchen, raids the cabinets, and starts his usual Saturday morning ritual the two of us enjoy when life is simple and we're not talking business and politics. He pulls down the Krusteaz pancake mix, grabs bacon and eggs from the fridge, and finds my bag of oranges so he can squeeze the life out of them the way we like.

"We have to think of something to say to the reporters. I'll call the Blue Willow Inn to let them know we're still on for the engagement party," he says as he plops eggs into the pancake mix.

"Light on the eggs, Lamonte." His back is turned to me, but I know his mind is moving at lightning speed. He hunches his shoulders as he stirs the mix. "You're about to face more scrutiny than you have in your life. Are you ready?"

"I don't want to be bothered with this today."

"I'll step out on the lawn after we eat and address the scavengers."

"Yes, after we eat," I say.

Lamonte prepares our plates and pours juice. "Everything will be fine. This will blow over before you know it."

The elephant in the room grows. My hands tremble and my knees bounce as I think of an explanation. I've lied so long I'm not sure what the truth looks like.

I sigh and ask, "Aren't you curious about the article?"

His face slackens as he sips juice. "If you want to explain, that's your choice. I find it hard to believe the woman I've loved the last five years would keep a secret this huge from me. I'm waiting to hear what the mix-up is."

Ouch. I face the man I love. The one I've only allowed a tiny glimpse into my world.

"I meant to tell you before the wedding, Lamonte. The opportunity never presented itself."

"You were willing to have a wedding without having your mother present?"

I nod.

"What else should I know about you? You told me your mother died."

I shift in my seat. My cottony mouth offers, "I was young when I moved to Atlanta. My family thought it would be good for me to have a break from my mother's episodes."

"Episodes?"

"She—"

Lamonte's phone rings again. The voice announces Brooklyn Lucille Dunlap. Lamonte answers on the second ring. He accidentally presses the speaker button—a knack I can't get him to shake—and his mother yells, "Where's the lunatic?"

Lamonte quickly takes the phone off speaker and steps away from me. I can't hear everything she says, but from her booming voice, I string together, "bad choice," "not wife material," and "crazy grandchildren."

Lamonte holds up his hand and says to his mother, "I'm a grown man capable of making my own choices. Goodbye, Mother!"

He joins me at the table again, picks up the *AJC*, and re-reads the article. I see disappointment in his face and reach across the table to caress his hands. He pulls away.

"For twenty-three years, you've lived in this city without driving a few towns over to see your mother who's institutionalized in a mental facility?"

"Lamonte—"

He reads from the article. "My family decided it was better to parcel my children out like land just because I lose my grip on reality sometimes. My own baby girl is a big-time architect in Atlanta and she won't come to see about me."

"Lamonte—"

He holds his hand up again and reads, "She is so ashamed of me she spells her business name like a man. She won't use the name me and her father gave her."

"Lamonte."

"Toni, you told me the reason you spelled your name *Tony* was because you didn't want to be discriminated against as a female architect."

"That is true. When people see the name Tony Williamson, they assume I'm a man and are willing to do business with me. Tell me you haven't noticed the shock in men's faces when they meet me for the first time."

"Toni, you've been in business five years. Everyone in Atlanta knows Tony Williamson. Your work defies gender. Even race. Who are you? Don't I deserve to know who I'm about to spend the rest of my life with?"

I've got nothing. There is nothing I can say to him to convince him how sorry I am.

"Did you ever try to reach out to your sister all these years?"

"I tried. No luck." I'll fix this lie later.

Lamonte clears our plates from the table in silence. A die-hard penny-pincher, he rarely uses my dishwasher. Says it's too expensive. Instead, he fills my sink with hot water, Dawn, and a capful of bleach and cleans the dishes. As if his scrubbing will wash away what is going on between us.

I join him at the sink, but he shoos me away, tells me to get ready for tonight. I gaze out the front window at my lawn; a few reporters remain.

I walk to my front door, yank the door open, stand in my robe and slippers and yell, "You are trespassing. Please leave the premises."